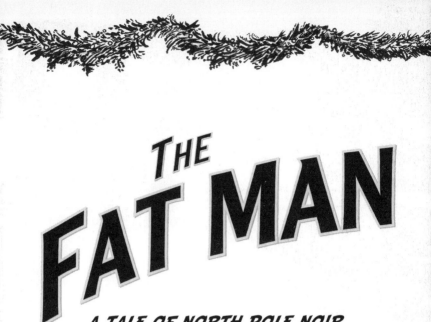

THE FAT MAN

A TALE OF NORTH POLE NOIR

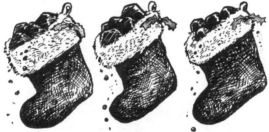

Ken Harmon

Dutton

DUTTON
Published by Penguin Group (USA) Inc.
375 Hudson Street, New York, New York 10014, U.S.A.
Penguin Group (Canada), 90 Eglinton Avenue East, Suite 700, Toronto, Ontario M4P
2Y3, Canada (a division of Pearson Penguin Canada Inc.); Penguin Books Ltd, 80 Strand,
London WC2R 0RL, England; Penguin Ireland, 25 St Stephen's Green, Dublin 2, Ireland
(a division of Penguin Books Ltd); Penguin Group (Australia), 250 Camberwell Road,
Camberwell, Victoria 3124, Australia (a division of Pearson Australia Group Pty Ltd);
Penguin Books India Pvt Ltd, 11 Community Centre, Panchsheel Park, New Delhi–110
017, India; Penguin Group (NZ), 67 Apollo Drive, Rosedale, North Shore 0632, New
Zealand (a division of Pearson New Zealand Ltd); Penguin Books (South Africa) (Pty)
Ltd, 24 Sturdee Avenue, Rosebank, Johannesburg 2196, South Africa

Penguin Books Ltd, Registered Offices: 80 Strand, London WC2R 0RL, England

Published by Dutton, a member of Penguin Group (USA) Inc.

First printing, November 2010

1 3 5 7 9 10 8 6 4 2

REGISTERED TRADEMARK—MARCA REGISTRADA

LIBRARY OF CONGRESS CATALOGING-IN-PUBLICATION DATA
has been applied for

ISBN 978-0-525-95195-7

Printed in the United States of America
Set in Minister Standard
Designed by Amy Hill

PUBLISHER'S NOTE

For my family

CONTENTS

contents

CHAPTER 1

Nutcracker

*T*he straight dope is that you don't want to get on the Naughty List. It's my job to make sure you don't want your moniker anywhere near it. And brother, I like my job. I like it a lot. If you decide to pout, shout and cry, I'll tattoo your mug with a rock that leaves a mark and stings all winter long. Lip off to parents and teachers, and I'm the one coming down the chimney, loaded for bear. Go ahead and roll the dice with lying, cheating and pitching hissy fits. I'll be there Christmas Eve to make sure you take your lumps.

Of coal.

Don't believe me? You should ask Raymond Hall Junior about his coal collection. Cain, Mordred, Lizzie Borden—none of these tykes could hold a sickle to Ray

the Deuce. If little Ray had a guardian angel, we'd find her in a ditch, coldcocked by her own halo with Raymond's prints all over the gold. The kid's not completely to blame, I guess. Raymond Junior was an alum of the Naughty List, ignored and pushed down the primrose path by a dad whose own flaws launched more headaches than an ugly husband. I was never really able to get Raymond Hall Senior's attention, and that stuck to me like cold on a Cratchit. I wanted to make up for it with Raymond Junior.

Plus the little punk had it coming.

I mean, cats aren't supposed to be painted purple. Whoopee cushions have no business in a church pew. A kindergarten teacher shouldn't limp and sleep with the lights on for the rest of her life because of a student. But Raymond Junior managed to pull off all those capers in just one week. And the bad news was that, according to the Naughty List, he was having a slow week.

Now, Raymond's supposedly dreaming of sugarplums, but the smart money would be he's dreaming of grenades or giving an old lady a spider. Even asleep, he has that smirk on his face, like he's proud that he just made the Public Enemies list. We see him when he's sleeping. We know when he's awake. And we see that smirk a lot. Like father, like son.

From little Raymond's room, I slipped down the hall

to the den where the Christmas tree is battle-scarred and praying for January. Sleeping Beauty back there has used the once-proud balsam as an evergreen piñata since Thanksgiving. He's swatted the red glass balls off the branches with a spatula. He pushed the tree over once so he could decapitate a gingerbread man and another time to give the angel topper a mustache. His last attack was flinging his dinner onto the tree and spaghetti tinsel is as ugly as it sounds. After all that, the little hoodlum still had the cheek to hang a stocking up over the fireplace.

To an elf with a sack full of coal, that kind of chutzpah is answered with a little rock and roll.

Later, I went back so I could be there when he woke up, because this year, Raymond Junior really thought he was going to beat the system. At first light, he roared down the hall, a tornado in footie pajamas, but he went silent as a grave when he came into the den.

The space under the tree was empty. There was no fire truck. There was no checkerboard or football. And you'd have to be a damn fool to give this kid the bow and arrow and tomahawk set he craved. He'd restage the Donner Party right there in the cul-de-sac.

Raymond Junior stared slack-jawed at the tree skirt, empty except for a few stray needles and spaghetti sauce stains. But he didn't panic yet, not this kid. He looked to the hearth and could tell by the bulge that something was in his stocking. He ripped it off the nail and slammed his greedy little hand into the bottom of the sock.

I couldn't help but smile a little when he fished out a grimy, messy, ugly lump of coal. Again.

Raymond was numb with disbelief. He turned the lump of coal over in his palm several times as if he wondered if it would change into something else. He rubbed it and mumbled a wish. But all he got for his trouble was two dirty hands instead of one.

And that's when he started to cry. It was about time. At first, he just leaked a little, but then the pipe burst. Tears poured out of his beady little eyes and more liquid regret oozed out of his nose. A tissue was not going to do him any good. This kid was going to need a sponge. He cried and cried, choked a little on his tears and then,

"NOOOOOOOOOOOOOOOOOOOOO!"

Finally, Raymond Hall Junior was experiencing heartbreak and the shame that it was all his doing. Maybe, just maybe, he might remember the next time he thought about doing something he shouldn't. He'd remember this feeling and think twice about pulling the school's fire alarm or bullying the scrawny kid with an overbite. Now he'd learn his lesson or it would be worse the next time. I knew this was true because he kept crying and crying and crying. It was a great day.

Ho ho ho.

But things wouldn't stay jolly for long.

I didn't know it yet, but someone back at the North Pole was about to start playing reindeer games for keeps, gunning for the Fat Man and all the good things he stood for. It wouldn't be long before I was given the powder, fired, Old Yeller time. Santa gave me my walking papers and told me that there was a new elf in Kringle Town. He said that my kind of elfing wasn't needed anymore, that it was old hat. I didn't even get a fruitcake. It looked like my only friends at the moment were a bar stool at the Blue Christmas and a half-empty bottle of brown nog. Those two chums kept me from clearly seeing the doom-screaming headline:

THE MARSHMALLOW WORLD GAZETTE

Gumdrop Coal Fired from Coal Patrol
Santa's Dark Elf Is Out on His Ear

For a little while, things seemed too foggy even for Rudy's schnoz and the whole tale was about to get more twisted than a cheap string of lights, but I'm getting ahead of myself. I thought my bad luck started when I was put out to pasture, but now I know I was knee-deep in trouble long before that night.

So was Santa.

So was Christmas.

I didn't help matters any acting like a damn fool. I slapped some jaws, hurt some friends and broke some hearts, but that wasn't the worst of it.

The worst was the murder.

CHAPTER 2

I'm Telling You Why

I should back up a minute because there are some things you need to know. For instance, even though we work for Santa, an elf's DNA is not automatically dialed for sugarplums and fa-la-la-la. Not all elves are North Pole Moonies, saluting the flag and drinking the nog-aid. Some of us have been with Santa from the beginning, when St. Nick was strictly mom and pop, a grassroots happy-fest started by a fat kid and some sawed-off toy makers. We shared Santa's belief that there should be at least one night when children smiled. "A child gave the world so much that night in Bethlehem," Santa said. "I just want to find a way to spread the spirit of that wonderful gift!" I still choke up at the simple beauty of the Fat Man's notion. Elves are naturally nostalgic, but Christmas really was better back then. The giving came from the heart, but so did the receiving. The gratitude was genuine and the kids were really, truly thankful. But then the snake eventually brought his bag of apples to the Garden of Christmas, and after a couple of bites into the old McIntosh, the kids demanded more.

And old St. Nick couldn't—or wouldn't—say "no."

That's when the whole bag went south for some of us at the North Pole. Some elves couldn't stand to see the Fat Man kill himself trying to fill a black hole of greed. Some of us got dark. Some of us got bitter.

I got revenge.

Gumdrop Coal is my name and I'm a 1,300-year-old elf and the chip on my shoulder will give you tetanus. I'm two-foot-three, but if you think you can crack wise about my height or take me in a fight, you'll be making the worst mistake of your sorry life. I will jingle your bells up through your giblets hard enough to make your eyes scream.

I'm serious.

Remember that, and you and I will get along swell.

Here's what else you need to know. I wasn't always this jaded. I got a heart, but it's a hard one. My pop was the crabby dwarf from the old Snow White yarn. The old man had a real cob up his hinder and was meaner than the devil with a rash. When the Grimm boys first came around digging up dirt on the dwarfs and Snowy, Pop wasn't bashful about showing the brothers a fit that would shame a Viking. Pop held a torch for Snow, so when she gave him the old heigh-ho for that tall glass of Prince Charming, Pop added brooding to a bad temper. That Walt guy's picture of Pop was a pipe dream, and whatever was in the pipe was pretty rooty-tooty.

Mom was one of those stepsisters you heard stories about. For years, she thought she was the cat's meow until the woodland vermin decided to give her little half sister a makeover. The kid cleaned up pretty well and when she arrived at the ball looking like a million bucks, my mom and aunts looked like they had swallowed moat water. The prince asked the little half sister if she was the kind of girl who wanted to see his tower and, well, the shoe fit. Mom was not a bit happy about getting the short end of the slipper for a husband. To make matters worse, Mom's happily-ever-after story was having her eyes pecked out by ravens. She married Pop out of necessity, so she wouldn't run into the furniture. At the altar, Mom said, "I gotta marry somebody, so it might as well be a half-pint jerk weed." Mom resented Pop's crush on Snow and drummed on the old man's brow on the subject like an Apache on the warpath. She was none too pleased to be the runner-up to another "perfect" princess. Mom never let Pop forget how lucky he was to have her. Mom reminded the old man that she was only about three corns away from donning a glass slipper. If she would have had a little lanolin or a crowbar, she would be sitting on the throne.

"You'd be wiping my behind," Mom would screech from her stool in the corner. "You'd be no more than a lackey, a serf, a little fool with bells on your hat. You'd have to make me laugh or die."

"I wipe your behind now," Dad would thunder back. "I wait on you hand and foot, treat you like a queen, and you couldn't hold a candle to Snow White."

"I'm blind, you ignorant, pathetic little peckerwood!" Mom fumed through fake tears, trying to muscle up a little sympathy. "You owe me. Girls like your precious princess are heartless harpies who send their little animal friends out to prey on innocent people like me. They're vindictive little tarts is what they are. And don't kid yourself, stretch. Snow would have laughed you out of the bedchamber. You can't cross the moat with a sapling! Ha ha *ha*!"

Now you can see why I had to leave home.

Truth is, there aren't that many places in the world for elves to go. Despite what you may have read, Middle Earth is really for outlaws. Middle Earth elves and dwarfs are desperadoes who are looking for a hole to hide in and maybe score a quick treasure. They sit around and brew hooch from roots, scheming and plotting on how to survive another day. You really don't want to be in Middle Earth after dark, not if you want to keep your magic dust—or your throat.

Now if you are a sick little jasper, you can be an Old Country Elf. These are your basic leprechauns, dwarfs, gnomes, gremlins, pixies and hobs—mischievous, twisted little pucks with a knack for jerking around weak-minded humans too dumb to come out of the rain. Old Country Elves can make a living, but you're always on the job and working around werewolves, ogres and a long line of moor-inspired nightmares, so life is no picnic. Plus the food doesn't get much better than haggis, and there just isn't enough mead to wash that taste out of your mouth.

Munchkins are elves, but they'll try and tell you different. Munchkins are elf elitists, and if their Lollipop Guild puts the kibosh on your application, they'll pretend they never knew you. Personally, I never understood the attraction of being a Munchkin. They make their life sound all yippy skippy and ding-dong the witch is dead, but they don't tell you the Flying Monkeys are still around. I hear those ape-vultures drop out of the sky like the Angel of Death and sweep up a Munchkin in a blink. It's Flying Monkey takeout and I hear the leftovers look like the butcher's floor. If that's the good life, they can have it.

Some elves go rogue and strike out for your world, the human world. They try to pass themselves off as "little people," but some elfin birthmarks (the pointy ears and chins, the curled toes), usually give them away. The elves that happen to make do in your neighborhood are usually starring in freak shows and small-time circuses, and you don't need me to tell you how tough a carny's life is. It's hard work, dangerous. And there's no dental insurance.

The only other path for an elf to pursue is the North Pole, the show. It is the best, too, and it was the only path I had in mind.

I arrived at the North Pole in 725 A.D. on a winter morning colder than a snake's shoulder. I was a kid then, a little soft in the head and running from a hard home. I heard about a place of light and cheer and joy and I wanted to see if it was real. I heard about a guy—Nick to some, Kris to others—who was living to make children feel special. I wanted to be a part of something like that. I wanted to be moved before it was too late. I wanted what every kid wants—his wish to come true.

It only took a little over a thousand years. I just wished I could have gone a different way, that's all.

CHAPTER 3

Yes, Virginia

Before we get to how I got fired and all the mess that follows it, let me tell you how I got the job. Realize that there are some who wouldn't want me to spill about some of what goes on in Kringle Town. They don't want you to know that sometimes there's a rat in the figgy pudding. They want to keep secret some of the stuff that goes on behind gingerbread doors, but for the love of Christmas, I'm going to sing. Sue me.

The first fact you should know is that some elves have superpowers. From Santa to the lowliest stocking stuffer, there are special elves that have more moxie, more mojo, more brains and brawn and je ne sais quoi than any of those rubes in a cape ever hoped to have. Some of us can fly. We can shoulder a two-ton sack of toys without a grunt. Elves can turn invisible, throw our voices, breathe underwater, dance with fire and whistle through peanut butter. Elves cobble the toys, pepper the mint and deck the halls. We cast spells, raise hell and take names. You don't see us unless we want you to and then you don't recognize us. We can take your best shot and give it right back, but the point is moot. You'd never catch us or come close to landing a punch. Elves are smarter than you, quicker. Special. There is no kryptonite.

If you make it to the Pole and are discovered to have a super elf power or two, you're invited to a special training corps to learn how to use them, courtesy of Zwarte Piet, or Black Pete as he is sometimes called. Black Pete is one of Santa's right hands, a surly little flunky who was with him at the beginning and is tasked with creating an elite squad of Santa Helpers. Black Pete's academy is an elf gulag, a soul-sapping regimen of pain and ruin, with three meals a day of nothing but fruitcake and water. Black Pete's methods are meant to break you, and many are happy to get broken. But when you're broken is when you learn. You learn how to harness your magical elf powers, how to do push-ups with your gray matter. Delivering presents to the world in a single night would be quantum cyanide for most physicists, but Black Pete shows you the tune and teaches you how to play it so you really can help Santa.

Graduating a Zwarte Pieten means you know your onions. You get plum assignments like the toy line or chimney reconnaissance. You race reindeer and go undercover to check The List. Twice. A Zwarte Pieten is an elf rock star. But if Black Pete spits a line of gingerbread juice in your general direction, it's curtains. Peter out and your job is trying to match all the abandoned and lost socks of the world or raking out reindeer stalls. It ain't pretty. Santa's reindeer get a lot of fiber. A lot.

The other poop you need to be wise to is that our world, Kringle Town, is in a different dimension than your human world, hovering at the edge of what you can see and hear. Kringle Town is always there, just out of sight. It's how we see you when you're sleeping, know when you're awake. It's how we know if you've been bad or good—well, you know the rest. Kringle Town is full of smaller cities and burgs, rivers, oceans, the works. We even have an "other side of the tracks" and I shouldn't have to tell you it's called Pottersville, and you don't want to go there unless you want some bad business. Kringle Town's population is all your favorite holiday characters. We don't just come to life after Halloween. We all have lives to live and jobs to do here throughout the year, so our day-to-day resembles yours in a way. Your world doesn't have as much snow, and the Muzak isn't cranking out carols 24/7, 365 days a year, but we have a lot more in common than you think. The point I want to make is the holiday characters that you know and love can have bad days too, from low blood sugar (a real problem despite all the candy), to the stress of trying to stay chirpy for the cause. I mean, Frosty is real. I see him all the time in that old silk hat he found. But the Snowman likes to travel, and when he goes south, Frosty puddles in a skinny minute. Now, say you're minding your own business and happen to step into that puddle. Well, friend, you're going to get an earful from a voice at the bottom of your shoe that will tell you just how intimately you can get to know a carrot if you don't get your curly-toed boot out of his face.

That's just how it is some days. It's not all lollipops and root beer. We've got baggage. You need to understand that, stomach it. If you don't think you can take knowing that some of your holiday buddies occasionally pull on the cranky pants, you need to stop reading pronto. If you're too sentimental about the characters you've heard about since you were in footie jammies, then this tale ain't gonna be your cup of cocoa. It gets ugly. It will shake your snow globe.

On the other hand, it's a great yarn, even if I do say so myself.

Last warning.

Okey-doke, let's go to school.

I owe Black Pete. The old Zwarte-Master took me under his wing at the beginning and practically raised me as his own. When I shuffled into Comet Hall that morning at the North Pole, I was a down-on-my-luck kid who just fell off the turnip wagon, and was more than a little lost. Santa, who has a soft spot for just about everyone, put his arm around me and said, "Gumdrop, I believe your slight frame carries a great prize inside, but we need to build you up a smidgen to help you lift. My friend Black Pete can help you, I think. He may growl like a polar bear, but I have a feeling Zwarte Piet is just what you need." With that, Santa escorted me over to his gnome commando.

My first look at Black Pete made me swallow my gum. He was a couple of bumps above four feet tall, a giant in the elf world, and as solid as a Yule log. Pete had lost an eye as a young doughboy in the great Pixie Coup of 17 A.D., so his patch and the rest of the scars let you know that crossing this elf was the wrong way to dance. Black Pete would focus his good eye on your sorry self, twist you like a pretzel with a glare and find your every flaw. He'd snort and huff like he hated the sight of you. "What's this, Kris?" he asked Santa while he glowered at me. "You taking out the trash?" Black Pete's voice sounded like a hurricane waking up on the wrong side of the devil.

"Now, Pete," Santa said. "Holly Jolly, please. Black Pete, I'd like you to meet Gumdrop Coal. He arrived today and I think he just may have a place with us here."

The old musketeer cocked another cold stare my way and spit. "It ain't the time to be taking on charity cases, Kris. We need elves that are ready to work now. I ain't got time to babysit some fool pumpkin roller."

At that moment, Black Pete sounded like an echo from home and my spine went straight. "I don't know what you think you see with that lonesome peeper of yours, mister, but I can take anything you care to dish out and then some," I said before I thought better of it.

Black Pete rolled the plug of gingerbread chaw around his cheek and studied me, trying to ignore the twinkle in Santa's eye. Black Pete shot a stream of reddish ooze at my shirt, but I didn't move a muscle. I knew what he was doing. Then Black Pete smiled. A big smile, like a sunrise. He put a huge arm around me and said, "Kris, let me see what I can make of this boy. Follow me, son."

That's exactly what I did. I followed Black Pete like a son, letting him be the father I always wanted. I sponged every lesson he spilt, listened to every word he said. He never went soft on me. He worked me harder than any other Zwarte Pieten cadet, but when I pulled the blanket up to my chin at the end of the day, sore and beat, I knew I was cared for. And that made for easy dreaming.

I won't kid you, Zwarte Pieten training was rough as a scab most days, but without it, I wouldn't have gained a father, a purpose, or my best friend—Dingleberry Fizz. Dingleberry Fizz and I met that first week of boot camp. Black Pete was trying to teach us how to fly by putting us at the bottom of an avalanche. The old man stood at the top of a mountain and kicked boulders down the hill until they started to take some of their friends with them. About six of us stood quaking in our curled boots at the bottom of the mountain as rocks the size of battleships rolled down on us. Elf flying is all about willpower and focus, seeing yourself in the air. Black Pete trained you by giving you the choice of seeing yourself getting squashed like a bug by a rock or soaring above it. As the first boulder approached, our unknown instinct kicked in and all six elf cadets went to the air. It was more like a big jump rather than a launch, but Black Pete knew that as he pitched rocks at us, we'd either get the hang of flying or we wouldn't, so he pitched rocks at us with deadly accuracy.

So there I am dancing just above the avalanche, trying my best to overcome the notion of gravity. After half a minute, I was exhausted, my brain already sapped from trying to focus on flying. I was flapping in the air, but could feel myself drifting down. I looked up and a stone as big as the moon was coming straight toward me. I thought I was a goner, but suddenly something snatched my hand and yanked me up over the big stone and high above the rumble of the avalanche. My rescuer was a fair-haired elf with a long, straight nose and the reddest cheeks I'd ever seen. He had bright blue eyes and a kind of crooked half smile. "Squeeze your hinder," he said to me.

"What?"

"When I squeeze my hinder together, it helps me concentrate on flying better," he said. "I don't know why, but it does." Just to prove it, he darted straight up in the air, looped upside down and cruised back beside me pretty as you please. I could feel myself drifting back down, so the elf gave me a small kick in the behind and said, "Try it."

The kick helped. I squinted and kind of folded my backside into itself. It was a different sensation, though not a completely uncomfortable one. My mind wandered into trying to figure out the reason you'd want to do such a thing with your body, when suddenly I started to fly. I mean, I really flew. The guy was right; twisting up your cheeks kind of cleared your mind and then your inner pilot was allowed to take the controls. Suddenly, flying was as natural as falling off a log, and I skipped across the sky like a dove, my new friend right beside me.

"Thanks," I said, extending a hand. "I'm Gumdrop Coal."

"Dingleberry Fizz," he said. "Don't mention it. It's why I'm here."

That simple statement is what best describes Dingleberry. He is the sweetest soul I know. You can't get him down, can't make him mad. The light is always on. The first thing Dingleberry thinks about when he wakes up in the morning is helping somebody out. He can't wait to get started, either. He usually is up and at 'em at the crack and ready to go without a drop of coffee. You'll be kidnapped from a dream by Dingleberry standing at your bunk, shaking you and smiling. "Hey, wake up! Slingshot Ruthie needs a new coat of sprinkles on her house! Want to go with?" he'd ask, all excited. If you rolled back over, Dingleberry didn't judge. He'd be back in an hour or so as you pried your eyes open. "Now that you're up, let's go learn how to make doll heads, so we can help when the girls get behind." Even when I got into one of my foul moods and growled that I had my job to do and didn't have time or even the inclination to help someone else, Dingleberry just smiled patiently. "You don't mean that, deep down," he'd say, believing it. "You're just tired. Just try and think Holly Jolly thoughts and you'll be OK."

It was hard to stay mad at the world with a friend like Dingleberry Fizz. He is the elf I've always wanted to be. I asked him once what made him so happy and he blushed and said, "You promise not to laugh?"

I promised and Dingleberry shyly pulled out a copy of Kringle Comics from his vest pocket. "Him," he said. "I want to be like my hero." He held the comic book so I could see the cover, where a strapping beanpole of a man swung out of the shadows of a dark street lassoing a cloaked figure with one hand and ringing a small bell with the other. In big letters, the title screamed:

BY GEORGE ADVENTURES
BELLS AT MIDNIGHT!

Despite the danger, the hero had a sunny disposition and the word balloon coming from his smiling face read, *"Dog-gone it, Potter, ring the bell why doncha?! Why we give out wings all the time back in Bedford Falls!"* Without thinking about what I was saying, I asked Dingleberry, "You read this junk?"

Not only did Dingleberry read *By George Adventures*, the derring-do exploits of the old Building and Loan pal turned swashbuckler were what Dingleberry lived for. He kept each comic book issue sealed in plastic. He had action figures. He organized comic conventions and costume contests. Dingleberry was a one-man *By George* fan club. Dingleberry even believed the George tales were real. No one had seen old moth-back George in years. Back before my time, George was a regular in Kringle Town, but now he was long gone and probably dead. There were a lot of stories, but that was all. To a lot of us, George was no more real than his statue in Kringle Town Square. It's hard to believe in a legend covered with partridge poo, but that didn't stop Ding and the legion of "By George-a-teers" from chasing down every rumor of their hero's existence. There were hundreds of books on the subject, some claiming that George was a super spy or was fighting monsters over in Halloween City. Elves called into late-night radio shows and whispered that they had seen George flit by in the shadows, dashing off somewhere to protect Christmas spirit and the wonderful lives it inspires. Because of these yarns, Ding believed and tried every day to be as brave and happy and selfless as his hero. It was crazy, but I couldn't help but love Dingleberry more for it.

Dingleberry and I remained best pals, even though our jobs took us in different directions. The first few hundred Christmas Eves were no big deal. The world was smaller then and no one, especially kids, had much to speak of. It was pretty simple for Santa to swoop in and out and leave a loaf of bread or a bag of potatoes at the door. Then Nick would leave a piece of candy for the kid and everybody was happy. A few centuries later, Santa got the idea to give the kids toys, and that's when the elf corps started to grow. Santa needed elves to find the really deserving kids, the ones with good hearts, and who better than Dingleberry Fizz? Pretending he was costarring in an issue of *By George*, Dingleberry could go into the worst slum in the world and find a kid so good, so perfect, elves fought over who would actually get to make the toy for the kid. Dingleberry had a nose for good.

Me? I was different. It bugged me when kids tugged on Santa's beard like Quasimodo ringing for chow. I got steamed when they whined about what they didn't get. Every sass, fit and eye roll made me grind my teeth. I thought the kids were greedy and playing Santa for a sap. I had to do something.

I started the Coal Patrol.

CHAPTER 4

The Jingle Bell Rock

I guess the idea of naughty kids stuck in my craw from way back. Santa and the elves were busting it to make and deliver gifts to kids, even if they didn't deserve them, but the Fat Man would still keep them in the system. The Kringle Town network makes Big Brother look like small potatoes. We really can see everything. All year, we'd watch little Johnny give the devil to parents, teachers and siblings, but come Christmas morn, the squirt got a king's ransom in toys and candy, rewarded for the headaches he passed out during the year. It burned me, especially when kids started asking for more, expecting it. I thought they were getting a little big for their britches, so I had a heart-to-heart with Santa.

"Boss, I think we can teach these bad nippers a lesson if all we give them is a lump of coal for Christmas," I said. "Sort of fire a shot across the bow that they had better shape up."

Santa studied his cup of cocoa for a moment. "That seems a little cruel, Gumdrop," Santa said. "Some children simply don't know any better. They live in a hard world; they don't know another way to behave."

"Yeah, that's what Dingleberry says too," I answered. "He calls it 'context.' I guess he reads more than comic books. Anyway, I call it 'excuses.'"

"It may be an excuse, Gumdrop, to be sure. But do you really want to rob a child of a moment of joy? Do you want them to believe that there is nothing good? The Child we celebrate with our deeds grew up to hang out with some pretty despicable people just so He could show them how to believe in good," Santa said.

"Yeah," I replied. "And look what happened to Him."

"I do look at what happened to Him," Santa said seriously. "It caused something wonderful to happen to the world. What happened to Him resulted in hope for every one of us."

"Sorry, I stepped over the line, Santa," I said. "But even His book preached, 'Spare the rod, spoil the child.' I think my plan is kind of a gift too, Santa. It gives them the gift of knowing that they just can't do what they want. They will discover that what they do touches other people. Then they will learn they can make a difference, a good one. Learning that changing your ways is a gift to yourself and others is really something special, don't ya think?"

Santa nodded. "But why coal?" he asked with a smile.

"My name had nothing to do with it, I promise you. I just figured that coal is dirty and nasty, not a lot of fun, but the family could use it to keep warm."

"And that the lump of coal represents the Child," Santa said. "A beautiful diamond is hidden inside."

That was the furthest thing from my mind, but I'd go with it to get my way. "Now you're getting it," I said.

It took months to talk Santa into it. He really didn't think it was right. But after weeks of badgering, Santa said, "I will allow it. Since you seemed to have already discussed this with Dingleberry, I imagine that you two have figured out how to determine which children receive coal."

"We're adding a report to the Naughty List," I said. "I'll have my recommendations based on mine and Dingleberry's research, but you'll have the final say, sir."

"Do you really think this will work, Gumdrop?"

"Yeah, Kris, I do. Someone is going to learn a lesson."

Boy, would they.

Anyhow, that's how the Coal Patrol got started. We were small at first; just me and a couple of other elves dropping a few rocks here and there. Most of the kids seemed to get the message, and Santa saw the value of that. He kept us on a short leash, but let us keep the shop open. It was good work, but not what I'd call pleasant. No matter how rotten the Raymond Halls of the world are, there's nothing fun about watching a kid be disappointed on Christmas morning. Remorse is a tough knot for a kid, but when they get it, they get it, and you've done them and the world a favor. Over the years, some kids stayed rotten. Raymond Hall and Junior, for example. But we turned around some kids, got them to smell the coffee and really and truly reflect the Christmas spirit. Those successes made me proud. Well, you know what goes before the fall.

THE MARSHMALLOW WORLD GAZETTE

Gumdrop Coal Fired from Coal Patrol

Santa's Dark Elf Is Out on His Ear

By Rosebud Jubilee

Veteran disciplinarian elf and founder of the Coal Patrol, Gumdrop Coal, is out on his pointy ear, relieved of his duties yesterday. According to sources, Coal had become too zealous in his punishing of children. The list of tykes getting only a lump of coal on Christmas morning had grown to unacceptable levels, said some. "Gumdrop was shelling kids like peanuts," said Zwarte Piet, the famous elf trainer. Piet was also a personal mentor to a young Coal. "It's sad because the program had merit, but old Gumdrop got full of too much starch for some people's liking. Coddling kids seems to be the school of thought and unloading a bunch of rocks on a kid is not the message we need to be sending, I guess." Charles "Candy" Cane will head the Coal Patrol effective immediately. "I am honored with this appointment from Santa," Candy Cane said. "While discipline is indeed an important buttress of the message we want to convey, I feel the previous administration of this office took things too far. His targets were children, after all, and they, of all beings, should be afforded more compassion and mercy. As my grandmother used to say, 'Candy, you get a lot more with honey than you do vinegar.' I look forward to instituting a new standard for influencing naughty children in the future. One with more honey and no vinegar, and certainly no coal."

Gumdrop Coal could not be reached for comment.

You're darn tootin' I couldn't be reached for comment. I was in no condition to comment. I was perched on the last stool in the dark corner of the Blue Christmas trying on a few cups of cheer. Doubles. Elvis, the Blue

Christmas's garçon, was pouring steady, but I could still feel the bite of Candy Cane's words and the sting of getting dumped by Santa. Cane had something to prove; he was a real comer. He got in Santa's ear and the old man listened. I understood that Santa didn't want to make a kid sad, but I thought my years on Coal Patrol gave me more credit with him. I hurt all over. When I took a second to stop feeling sorry for myself, I noticed good old Dingleberry was there to try and keep me company, but I really just wanted to be alone.

"Why don't you go home, Dingleberry? I'll be fine," I said. "Besides, you don't want to be seen with the likes of me. It could be a career killer if any of Cane's minions see you hanging out with the elf who hates kids."

"No one thinks that, Gumdrop," Dingleberry said with a smile. He was always with a smile. "And I'm here because you're my friend. At the end of the day, elves are here to help each other. Cane's not going to punish me because you're my friend."

"You really believe that?"

"I do," Dingleberry said.

"Huh. Next you'll be telling me those *By George* tales are real," I said. Being the prince that he is, Ding ignored the knock. "I thought I was doing a lot of good, but I guess that's what I get for thinking," I said, motioning Elvis to pour me another. Dingleberry shook his head no at the barkeep, but I said, "Ignore him, Elvis.

I'm all shook up, but one more cup should steady me."
Dingleberry's shrug gave Elvis the green light and the
little man poured. "You're a good elf, Elvis," I said.

"Thank you, thank you very much," he said, giving
me a chuck on the shoulder before he sauntered down
to the other end of the bar. Dingleberry and I sat quietly for a moment, but too much silence was heavy on
my friend. "It really will be all right, Gumdrop."

"Will it?" I asked. "The Coal Patrol is all I've known
for hundreds of years, Dingleberry. It's all I've ever done.
We did good work. We taught some kids a lesson."

"A hard lesson."

"Those are the only kind worth learning, bub," I
said. "And now it's over. It'll end up killing Santa, you
watch. Look at him. He's working himself to the bone
pleasing the good kids. Can you imagine how worn out
he's going to be once those greedy little brats realize they
can get anything they want? The greed machine will go
into high gear."

"Don't talk like that," Dingleberry said. "Santa will
be fine."

"Look at the dark circles around his eyes," I said. "Already, it looks like he's wearing a mask. The Fat Man's
losing weight, Dingleberry. He's wearing stomach pad-
ding like a dime store Santa. I bet he don't weigh eight
stones wet. This will be the end of him, I bet you."

"Can I quote you on that, Uncle?" said a voice behind me. I turned to see Rosebud Jubilee, the pip-squeak reporter from *The Marshmallow World Gazette* rag. Rosebud was a crackerjack little thing; her red hair was a waterfall of crimson confection and the freckles on her nose and cheeks looked as good as sprinkles on an ice cream cone. She wore a purple hat because she liked wearing it. It looked a little ridiculous, but the angle of the chapeau told you she didn't give a hoot about what you thought. A peppermint stick dangled from her lips, bouncing up and down as she talked like a conductor working up steam for the finale. She looked at me with a little smirk behind the peppermint, like she had me all figured out. I didn't mind as much as I should have. It was a nice kind of smirk.

"Never believe anything you hear in the Blue Christmas, sister," I said. "Didn't they teach you that in Hack Reporting 101?"

"I cut class that day," she said, hopping up on the stool beside me without being asked. "I was on a story about some kid that locked himself in the closet because Santy Claus kissed him off with a bag of coal."

"Maybe the kid was naughty."

"Maybe the kid just needed a spanking."

"Maybe that's what I gave him."

"Maybe you were too rough."

"Maybe you'd like to find out."

"You gonna bend me over your knee, Gumdrop?" she asked.

"Maybe."

"Are you still on the clock or you just trying to get on the Naughty List yourself?" Her smirk was now a smile. Round One, Rosebud—a knockout. I could feel Dingleberry beside me turn as scarlet as Hester's monogram. "Elvis, the lady needs a cup of cheer. I imagine her mouth gets parched with as much as she talks."

Rosebud Jubilee pounded the bar. "Gimme a peanut butter and banana daiquiri, straight," she said. "And use the crunchy. Momma hasn't had breakfast." Elvis slid a mug of the house special to her and gave her a salute. She dispatched it in one gulp, wiped her pretty little mouth and dared me to say something else smart.

"Just so you know, all of that was off the record," I said. "Even though it was just for laughs." I was squirming a little, but I didn't want her to see it.

"Don't go and have kittens, Coal," she said with a warm smile. I liked the smile. "I'll get my story when it's ready. You got to thaw out a bit before I put you in the oven."

"Why not just throw me right into the frying pan?" I asked. "Everybody else has."

"Off the record and cross my little old heart," Rosebud said, "I think you got a raw deal."

"Your story didn't say as much," Dingleberry said from my elbow.

Rosebud sized Dingleberry up and decided to go easy on him. "The first rule of journalism, Mr. Fizz, is to meet your deadline," she said. "Your chum here couldn't be reached for comment. I looked under every rock I knew and, believe me, I know plenty. The boss wanted the story I had in my Royal typewriter so far and that's what got the ink. Now, if Gumdrop wants to tell me his side of the story, then I'm ready to listen."

"Don't do it, Gumdrop," Dingleberry said, suddenly worried. "It's a trick and you're in enough trouble already."

"Does he tuck you in too?" Rosebud asked me. There was that smile again. It was a nice smile.

"Only if I can't find somebody better," I said, trying my luck. She didn't slap me, so I gave Dingleberry the heave-ho. "Dingleberry, why don't you run along now. I appreciate you coming to see me, but I'm going to finish my chat with Miss Jubilee—it is Miss, isn't it?"

"Momma tucks herself in."

"I'm going to finish talking to her and then I'm going to go home and figure out what to do next," I said. "I'll be fine."

"But," Dingleberry said, scared.

"Really, Ding. Everything's gonna be all right."

Dingleberry chewed on it a half minute more and then slid off the stool. "You call me when you get home, OK? Please."

"I will. I promise. You run along now."

It was quiet for a minute after Dingleberry skipped off, as if Rosebud and me realized that we didn't deserve to know an elf as fine as Dingleberry Fizz. "He worries," I said finally.

"I gathered," she said. "I bet it's nice to have somebody worried about you."

"That would be a good bet," I said. "No one's worried about you?"

"No," Rosebud said, twisting the peppermint around her mouth. "I'm a snowflake in a blizzard. The only people who care about me are the housewives waiting for the next piece of gossip or the politicians who think I can turn their lies into lullabies. If I got run over by a reindeer tomorrow, nobody would miss me."

"Don't count on it."

"That's sweet, but I'm OK with the idea of it. It means I'm free to do what I want." Rosebud said it, but the silence behind it lacked her usual spunk. I filled it.

"So why you still circling this story, Jubilee?" I asked. "There's no more meat to it. I'm finished. End of story."

"I think you were set up," she said. "And I think you think it, too."

"Candy Cane," I said.

"Santa's bright boy."

"I don't doubt he bent the old man's ear," I said. "But I think he's just trying to make his mark. The Coal Patrol was the easiest target. Folks have been telling me I was too rough on kids for years. Santa still gets hate mail from the Raymond Halls of the world because of me. Maybe Santa thought it was time for a change."

"You don't think that," she said, leaning in. "You just said you thought that naughty and nice kids both getting presents would kill Santa. Now suddenly change is good? Tie that bull up outside, cowboy."

"Once Cane sees what spoiling all children will do to Santa, he'll pull back," I said. "I bet they'll just give a few less presents to the naughty kids. The point is that they don't want the kids to have their face rubbed in it, which is what a bag of coal does." Rosebud looked at me like I was selling cheese. I smiled and gave her hand a little pat. "Boy, your ribbons are tied too tight, honey, if you think Cane's out to get Santa. Without the big guy, we'd all be out of business. Why would he want Santa out?"

Rosebud moved her hand, but not right away, I noticed. "Maybe he thinks he could do the old man's job better," she said, spitballing. "He already thinks he can do your job better. Maybe Cane wants to run the show."

"That's a pipe dream," I said. "It'll never happen. The world would never stand for it."

"They would if they didn't have a choice."

The idea that somebody was trying to hurt Santa burned me, even if it was just a bunch of cockamamie bunk from a two-bit reporter in a purple hat. I got up to leave. "I feel sorry for you, Jubilee. It must be awful to have to try and sleep with those kinds of ideas in your head. Farewell, my lovely."

"You don't think it's possible?" she asked. "You're not going to do anything about it?"

"I am going to support Santa and the new Candy Cane Coal Patrol any way I can!" But the words didn't taste right in my mouth. Something in my gut told me that little Miss Know-It-All might be on to something, but I needed to go someplace where I could add things up.

"More bull," Rosebud called out after me. "You're a regular rodeo cowboy."

"No," I said, as I headed out the door. "I'm a regular misfit."

As I said it, I knew what I was going to do next.

CHAPTER 5

A Couple of Misfits

To: Coal Patrol Officers;
    Nice List Executive Committee
From: The Office of Charles Cane
Re: Toy Inspection

I first want to begin by saying that I am
deeply humbled to be serving as your leader
in our endeavor of providing children of the
world holiday joy. We have quite a challenge
before us, as Christmas will be here before
you know it and, per my appointment, we
will not be as strict in denying children
toys from their wish list. That means more
toys must be built, my wee ones, and I am
confident that you are up to the challenge.

With this increase in production, it is important that quality does not suffer. Not only will it hinder our ability to fulfill the wish lists of children all over the globe, but we also run the risk of overpopulating Misfit Isle by creating less than perfect playthings. To that end, Santa has asked that I personally inspect all toys before they are delegated to the appropriate child. Thank you for your cooperation in this matter and for your focus on this new holiday campaign. When we celebrate at the Loading of the Sleigh Parade Christmas Eve, you will have accomplished great things.

*T*he only way to get to the Island of Misfit Toys was by boat, and the only boat was a slow one, *The Scrooge*. Tiny Tim was the skipper, so the barge literally limped through the water. I'm not kicking the kid with a crutch; that was Tim's joke. Not too many ventured out to Misfit Isle and Tiny was starved for company. When he got a passenger for a crossing, Tiny Tim made the most of it. "We'll limp over to the island as quickly as we can," he'd say, giving the motor a gasp of fuel. "But Uncle Scrooge doesn't like me to waste fuel skipping across the water. Costs too much money. I fear a leopard can't change all of his spots." Then Tiny would settle in and ask you a million questions, do tricks with his crutch, anything for a little companionship. Tiny Tim was lonely, forgotten except when Christmas needed a sad, saintly cherub to tug at the heartstrings, but then folks moved on. Uncle Eb's comeuppance was where the scenery got chewed and the gimp tended to slow down the hamming. Tiny Tim was constantly being pushed to the side. Still, he seemed to take it in stride.

"Gumdrop, it is oh so nice to see you," Tiny said. "It truly is."

"Thanks, kiddo," I said. "How are you doing, Tiny? How's the boat business?"

"Oh, it is splendid!" he said. "As good a job as I could ever hope for, and much more than I deserve. Despite his grumbling, Uncle Scrooge really is very kind to give me this ship to captain."

"Seems to me a good kid like you deserves something with a little more dignity," I said. "You're the poster child for the Nice List."

"You are too kind, Gumdrop," Tim said. "But I really don't mind. In fact, with my withered leg and common crutch, I feel a true kinship with the Misfits. They too are crooked and broken, but, on the inside, giving and true of heart. A crust of love's bread is what we seek. If others are not able to share a crumb, at least we can share it with each other. It is an honor, truly, to do so with my Misfit friends."

"Tim, you're as good as gold."

"Now, now, you will make me blush," Tiny said. "So what brings you out to Misfit Isle?"

"I was thinking about seeing if they had any room," I said.

"Oh, I'm sure they'd be glad for the company, yes indeed," Tiny said. "But you are perfectly normal. It appears all your appendages are appropriately aligned."

"Maybe I just don't fit in at home," I said.

"I am sure you are loved more than you can possibly know."

"Always cheering the other guy up, aren't you Tiny," I said. "Are there any more of you? Do you ever get mad? Fed up? Ever want to take that stick you're leaning on and smack someone's kisser?"

My little speech embarrassed Tiny. He turned red and stared quietly out at the sea. "You must not think such things," Tiny said after a while. "If I were to have such a mean and hard heart, I would not deserve my many blessings. I would inherit Uncle Scrooge's other fate. I would belong to the ranks of Pottersville."

I laughed. "I could not ever imagine Tiny Tim in Pottersville, kiddo. Though your stick would come in handy when it came to cleaning someone's clock."

Tim turned away from me again.

"Sorry Tim," I said. "I didn't mean to upset you." We rode the rest of the way to Misfit Isle in silence.

It's not that the Misfit citizens were not hospitable or good company, but they were a moody bunch, especially where elves were concerned, so you never knew when your welcome would be worn out. At the end of the day, elves were responsible for the Misfits. The Misfits were there because some elf botched a design or a production plan, or simply came up with a really lame idea for a toy that the kids never cottoned to. When Santa saw that a toy could not be used, could not be loved, he would not deliver it on Christmas Eve, hurting a Misfit's feelings plenty. The island was home to thousands of toys that weren't up to snuff. Most were toy experiments, but sometimes dozens of botched toys were made before production was stopped. These "families" of toys tended to create their own neighborhoods on Misfit Isle, so they could easily share clothes and accessories. The one-offs were the free spirits of the island, the beatniks. They were the happier toys because they didn't round too many corners and see wrecked versions of themselves. In the beginning, Santa tried to let the Misfits live with everybody else in Kringle Town, but it was tough. Regular toys mocked the Misfits and made them feel like second-class citizens. Every few months, the Misfits would get fed up with the teasing and the stares and strike back at toys or even, out of frustration, at elves. Santa tried to pacify them in every way, but it got to where toys and elves and other folks in Kringle Town could not walk down certain streets at night safely, so Santa opened Misfit Isle. Santa thought he was creating a place where the Misfits could escape the teasing from other toys and have a better life. The Misfits saw it as banishment because an elf was stupid or incompetent. Santa hurt the Misfits' feelings, and the bitter seed took root. All in all though, life on the island was pretty good and most of the Misfits forgave, but didn't necessarily forget. You never knew when they would get prickly and strike back. You didn't want to be around then. When a toy has nothing to lose, he can be dangerous. I guess that goes for all of us too.

Still, I had friends there.

Sherlock Stetson and his Cow-Frau, Zsa Zsa, were a couple of toy disasters, but they were good eggs. A long time ago, cowboy and detective toys were all the rage, for both little boys and girls. One demented elf—Argyle Harmony, I think it was—got it into his pointy head to create a man and wife cowpoke sleuthing team, so little boys and girls could play together. Sherlock Stetson and Zsa Zsa were born. Unfortunately, something went squirrelly in the works, and Sherlock and Zsa Zsa came up short. For a master detective, Sherlock Stetson was kind of dim; he couldn't find a cow in a stampede. He had no talent for mysteries; most problems required him to lie down and take a nap. His dazed look and clueless phrases when you pulled his drawstring (*"Dern, if that clue had been a stampede, I'd be daid!"*) did not inspire children to play with him, and the half-ten-gallon/half-deerstalker cap adorned with bull horns made him look like an imbecile from a very bad opera. It didn't help that Sherlock Stetson also drooled. I think he was supposed to be able to spit "baccy juice," but his pucker had a sputter and the result was that Sherlock looked like he needed to be wheeled off to the dayroom for crafts.

Zsa Zsa Schnitzel was supposed to be Sherlock's funny and bright better half, firing up beans and kraut by the campfire to fuel Papa's deductive thoughts and rides to the rescue. However, because Sherlock's brain batteries were not included, she ended up having to take the crime-solving reins, and she didn't like the extra chores. Zsa Zsa was bitter about taking second billing to a husband she didn't want. "I vant to vatch zee crows eat zee brain outen his head," she'd say to anyone who'd listen. "If I have to solven another crime for him, I vill slit my throat wit a spur!" We elves did a little research and found that kids didn't want to play with the pair because the toys reminded them too much of their parents, minus the six-guns, lassos and language that would make the men of Tombstone gasp. Argyle tried to make them more appealing by giving the couple horses (Pudd and Clobber), but the result only made Sherlock and Zsa Zsa look like the sorry Horse-couple of the Apocalypse. Sherlock Stetson, Zsa Zsa and the rest of their bunkhouse buddies were banished to Misfit Isle without getting a real shot at playtime with kids, and that hurt them a little, I think. Well, it hurt Zsa Zsa. Sherlock forgot. Anyway, Sherlock Stetson and Zsa Zsa were permanent residents of Misfit Isle and my best friends there.

Years ago, Sherlock Stetson and Zsa Zsa helped me transition some Misfits who were going to be new to the island and we formed a good friendship. Even with the threats, the gouging, the broken crockery and the broken English, I enjoyed their company. I could count on Sherlock for a friendly face and simple advice, and Zsa Zsa was always good for a great meal and a kick in the pants.

I took a wobbly toy trolley car from the docks to the heart of Misfitville. The place hadn't changed much. Once you got past the shock of seeing toys with missing parts or too many parts, it looked like most any place in the world, except maybe this one was in need of some kind of telethon. Goo-spewing baby dolls cried in door stoops ignored by anatomically incorrect Malibu Sues who were watching their soldier and astronaut boyfriends put some "automatic kung-fu arm action" to the engine blocks of various broken vehicles. A few of them gave me the stink eye as I cruised by, but I felt safe. In the state I was in, I was one of them.

It took a few minutes for Sherlock to answer the door. Zsa Zsa screamed from the deep bowels of the bunkhouse, "Go answerin' zee door, you nincompoop!" A few minutes later, she said, "Zee *front* door, kraut for brains! Go to zee *front*!" I heard Sherlock pass by the front door a couple of times before he finally got a clue that he should open it. He seemed glad to have done so when he finally swung the door open and saw me standing there. "Why Lemondrop Coat, what a surprise," he said.

"Hiya, Sherlock. It's Gumdrop Coal, you remember me?"

"Why sure, Smallpox Cope, how could I forget you? C'mon in!" he said, leading me into the bunkhouse with a friendly hug. "It's been forever since we seen you last. I'm sure pleased you came to see us. Zsa Zsa will be so happy that you're here. I sometimes reckon she finds my company a mite tiresome."

As if on cue, Zsa Zsa burst into the hall from the kitchen. "Vhere in zee tarnation did you put zee eggs?! Were you trying to hatchen zem again?" she hollered, but stopped short when she saw me. Her eyes flashed red for a half a second and I thought I had picked the wrong day to be an elf. But then a sly smile snaked across her face. "Vell, if it isn't Gumdrop Coal!"

"No, it's Porkchop Hole, sweetie," Sherlock corrected her.

"Shut uppen before I kick you in zee chaps," Zsa Zsa

snapped. "I been listening datz you had some trouble, my vittle Gumdrop," she said to me. "A vittle trouble. It is good zat you come to talk to Zsa Zsa. I vill fix. Kitchen."

Those were marching orders, so I obeyed and followed her into a room of uncommonly good smells. Sherlock showed up a few minutes later, having forgotten to follow us. When he was glad to see me all over again, Zsa Zsa shoved a sausage in his mouth. "Quiet, idiot. Me and my vittle Gumdrop has to talk smart!" she barked.

"I can't believe the news about me getting canned traveled so fast," I said. "It's not that big a deal."

"It is large deal," Zsa Zsa said. "Now you are out vit Santa? Like a Misfit? Vhy? Zee fat man love the bad kinder, but can't find a place in his heart for Misfit Toys!"

"It seems that Candy Cane has a better way of handling things," I said. "And maybe he does, I don't know."

Zsa Zsa huffed. She began kneading a roll of dough like she was trying to tear the hide off an animal. "Candy Cane is impressive, yes," she said. "But me think he is not so smart to get my vittle Gumdrop fired. Are you sure you did not make Santa mad?"

"Not that I know of," I said. "I mean, Santa's always been a little uncomfortable with the idea of the Coal Patrol. He doesn't like to leave anyone out."

"Zat is not true," Zsa Zsa said, strangling the dough. "This island is full of toys he left out."

"Sorry, I meant kids."

"I know what you meant," Zsa Zsa said. "But it is not fair what he did to us, not fair. Misfit Toys vould be loved by some children if only Santa didn't spoil zem so vit perfect toys." She slammed the dough down, making sure it was dead. "What do you tink zis Candy Cane vill do?"

"I don't think he'll do much," I answered. "I think he'll give kids, good and bad, what they want, and that Santa will kill himself trying to please everyone, but that's just how Santa is."

Zsa Zsa stopped with the dough and gave me a level look. "Do you tink Candy Cane is trying to get Santa out of zee vay?" she asked. Rosebud asked more or less the same thing. Folks had way too much time on their hands, too much time to think.

"Not that I can tell," I said. "Why does everyone seem to think that Santa is in Cane's sights?"

"'Cause I hear that Cane heads up the Misfit Mafia," Sherlock said. I thought he had been asleep.

"What's the Misfit Mafia?"

"Rubbish," Zsa Zsa said, smacking Sherlock in the head with a rolling pin. "Sherlock, here, tinks he stumbled on a couple of Misfits who are planning to take over zee world vit dark, evil plans. Vhat he found vas a couple of Goodfella action figures throwing darts at a picture of Santa. Sherlock should take more naps."

"They told me Cane would get me if I tried to rustle them in," Sherlock said. "I believed them."

"Humbug!" Zsa Zsa said, smacking him again.

"So why were these toys throwing darts at Santa's pic?" I asked.

"Because der a couple of Misfits," Zsa Zsa said, shaking her head. "Ve all feel like dat from time to time. Santa vill never understand how much it hurts to be on zis island sometimes. He can see it vit kinder, lumping bad in vit good, but not vit toys. Sad, it is."

"Is that what you think he's doing by getting rid of me?" I asked. "Making bad children the same as good?"

"Ya, maybe."

"I never thought of it that way," I said, helping myself to a sausage. "And I don't like thinking about it that way, either."

"No?"

"No," I said. "Good kids aren't the same as bad kids and bad kids shouldn't get rewarded like they're good. Where's the justice in that? I don't like it."

Sherlock leaned in close and whispered, "I deduce that you're gonna do something about it, Bumdrop. Am I right?"

"Maybe."

Zsa Zsa gave the dough another lethal twist. "Be careful my vittle Gumdrop. Just be careful."

CHAPTER 6

Later On, We'll Conspire

THE MARSHMALLOW WORLD GAZETTE

Not So Wonderful Winter Wonderland

Police report that yesterday, Mr. Snowman was attacked. "We were just having fun with Mr. Snowman," said Wendell Spindle of Kringle Town, "and then these little hoodlums knocked him down." Witnesses were unable to give a clear description of the attackers, but some claim to have heard the gang yell, "The Fat Man is next! The Fat Man is next!" Santa said he was "disturbed" by the incident, but did not fear for his safety. If you have any information, please contact the Kringle Town police.

I stayed with Sherlock Stetson and Zsa Zsa for a couple of weeks, spending most of my time eating, refereeing their skirmishes, and trying to avoid being alone with Zsa Zsa. "I could make vittle Gumdrop happy," she said one night in the kitchen. I couldn't help but notice she was charring the bratwurst—or that Sherlock was sitting three feet away trying to grasp the idea of a yo-yo.

"You have a husband, Zsa," I said, trying to make a joke of it. "And I'm sure I would disappoint you."

"Sherlock, bah," Zsa Zsa said. "I'd rather have a Lincoln Log. Let's run away from zis Misfit place, Gumdrop. Even if I am a toy, I am all voman—no assembly required, eh?"

I left right after dinner that night.

When I got home, I found Dingleberry pacing in front of my door, in a dither. "Where have you been?" he said. I could tell the old boy had been crying. "You said you would call! You didn't call! I thought something bad happened to you!"

"I'm fine, Dingleberry," I said, motioning him in from the cold. "I spent some time over on the Misfit island. I just needed to get away. Thanks for worrying, though. What's the news here? Has Candy Cane conquered the world yet?"

Dingleberry's lips disappeared and his pupils got

glossy. "He told me that he was keeping an eye on me. He doesn't know if he can trust me because . . ." Dingleberry was scared to say more. I said it for him.

"Because of me. I'm sorry you got dragged into this, Ding. What happened?"

Dingleberry stared at the floor, ashamed to look at me. I guess he thought I would clobber him. I gave him a pat on the arm and made him look me in the eye so he would know everything was jake between us. "I don't know what happened," he said finally. "I went to see him about his toy reviews, and he started saying things like he had to be sure that he could trust me. He said he knew we were buddies, but that I had to put him and the mission first. Cane said if he ever felt that he couldn't trust me, he would fire me! Why would he say that, Gumdrop? Why? I *want* kids to have toys, as many as they deserve! I don't want any kids to get coal. No offense."

"None taken," I said, smiling and trying to calm Dingleberry down. "Did you talk to Santa?"

"I can't get a minute alone with him," Dingleberry said. "There have been threats, so Santa's surrounded by some of Cane's bodyguards. Plus, Santa's either creating new toys, building prototypes or recalculating his flight plans. He's too busy to talk to me."

"How's he look?"

Dingleberry was going to tear up again, so he turned away and didn't say anything. He didn't have to.

"Tell me something, Dingleberry, be honest," I said. "Do you think giving the naughty boys and girls toys makes them good little boys and girls? Makes everybody even?"

"I don't know, Gumdrop," he said. "That's one way to look at it."

"Another way to look at it is that it brings everybody down," I said. "There's no reward for good behavior. Anything goes. The kids who listened and did their homework are treated just the same as those who were throwing rocks at little old ladies. I don't think that's fair."

"There are a lot of things that aren't fair," Dingleberry said.

"Like you getting lumped in with me," I said.

Dingleberry shook his head. "No, that's different. Cane is doing that. He's being a bully. But I can't get fired, Gumdrop! I can't. If I don't get to give out toys I don't know what I'd do."

Dingleberry would curl up into a ball and roll away is what he'd do. I wasn't going to let him take the fall for me. "You're not going to get fired because you and I are no longer friends."

"Gumdrop!"

"We're no longer friends in Cane's eyes," I said. "Tomorrow night, you and I are going to have a big fight at the Blue Christmas. You'll give me the gate, but it will all be just for show, Ding, just for show. I will still love you like nobody else, but this spat will be our little secret, OK?"

The famous Dingleberry smile returned. "You mean like a game? Just like in *By George and the Adventure of the Tattoo Statue Switcheroo*! George let the Cannonball Cabal think they had stolen the famous, powerful statue Bisboo to give to the evil Potter, but George switched it!"

"Yeah," I said. "Just like that. And we'll play the game until everything calms down. Meanwhile, I want to see if I can find out how Cane's going to deal with naughty kids."

"Please be careful, Gumdrop," Dingleberry said. "I am not your father, so I can't tell you what to do, but please let Candy Cane deal with naughty kids. Cause trouble for Cane and other elves, but leave kids alone. Just stay away from the kids."

"Say that again!" Dingleberry did, word for word.

Bam! Dingleberry just delivered my Christmas present early, and it was exactly the right size. "Dingleberry, thank you. You have just given me a wonderful idea!"

"Oh, no!"

"Oh yes! And don't worry. I'm not going to mess with the kids."

Maybe it was how I should have been approaching things all along. On most of the Naughty List, the kids weren't the problem, the parents were.

Dingleberry and Santa were right when they said that most kids couldn't help being bad. That's because Mom and Pop didn't know how to keep a kid in line or simply didn't care. Yeah, maybe they were just doing the same thing their parents did to them, but son of a blitzen, they were old enough to know better now. And if they still didn't know, well, I decided I was going to change that.

The naughty kids who grew up to be naughty adults and raise more naughty kids were about to get a crash course in responsibility from the new, secret Coal Patrol.

I didn't need any help. I had elf superpowers, top-shelf Zwarte Pieten training and the freedom of not giving a damn. It was the only way I could save Santa from wearing himself out. It was the only way to pre-serve Christmas present justice. I figured it would stop any harebrained idea Candy Cane had and keep Dingleberry in the clover. If I couldn't teach the kids a les-son, I'd teach it to their no-good parents and make sure the lesson got passed on. That's the way it should have been in the first place.

Christmas Eve was still a few weeks away, so I had plenty of time. If Santa was going to deliver gifts to every kid, they were going to be good kids—their par-ents would make sure of it. The more I thought of the idea, the more I liked it, though I knew I couldn't tell anyone. Dingleberry would worry himself sick, Santa wouldn't approve and Cane would hang me like a stocking for such an idea, so I was going to keep my sweet little notion to myself.

I didn't need to look at the Naughty List to know which parent was going to get a house call first. He had been a lousy kid and, as a father, he wasn't giving his son a chance to be better. The coal warning I had delivered last year to the little squirt was forgotten by Groundhog Day when Raymond Junior celebrated the holiday by setting an actual groundhog loose during a ballet recital, turning *Swan Lake* into an ugly duckling quicker than you could say *tutu*. And Raymond Senior didn't even say a word to his son.

It was time to deck the Halls.

CHAPTER 7

Deck the Halls

THE MARSHMALLOW WORLD GAZETTE

Do You Hear What I Hear?

Gossip with Butternut Snitch

This issue, our Scuttlebutt Stocking is stuffed with rumors, hearsay and tales told out of school. First, something fishy is going on with a famous Myrrh-Maid. It seems the Myrrh maven is musing a scheme to turn myrrh into a new perfume! It sounds like someone's created Frankincense-stein! Next, nosy nightlife spies said a certain reindeer was really kicking up her hoofs recently at the Hustle & Bustle club. Witnesses say the little vixen staggered home, mumbling, "I'll never do that for two bucks again!" Finally, word has it that a BIG ELF ON CAMPUS has a bad case of puppy love for one of my fellow newshounds. Little snowbirds tell me that the lucky frail is covered in rosebuds, trinkets and candy canes because the chap thinks the she-porter is asking him all those questions for a personal purpose. Stay tuned!

After everything I had been through with Little Raymond, Raymond Hall Senior was the obvious choice for a visit. Big Ray was not going to win any parenting awards, because he had been such a rotten kid himself. When he was little, Raymond broke a bat on Johnny's head; somebody snitched on him. He hid a frog in his sister's bed; somebody snitched on him. With each sin, somebody stooled on Raymond, and, every Christmas morning, Raymond had more coal in his stocking than a West Virginia miner. But Raymond didn't learn. As he got older, his crimes went beyond putting tacks in the teacher's chair and tying knots in Susie's hair. Raymond got into cheating on exams, putting sawdust in the gas tanks of enemies and slipping Mickeys into a coed's beer. Raymond's sins continued when he became a titan of industry, pioneering the on-hold messaging business. Not only did he send up the blood pressure of anyone who had ever been put on hold and had to listen to some canned ad of baloney instead of a live person, Raymond ran Don't Hang Up with the scruples of a raccoon. Profits were high, wages were low and dames in the office had more fingerprints than the glass on a candy case.

Raymond married Cynthia, a college sweetheart who didn't focus on Raymond's shortcomings because the monkey on her back kept her eyes blurry. Together, they birthed Little Ray. Raymond's interest in his son ended at the first dirty diaper, causing the poor kid to grow into a completely charmless cherub who deserved to be beaten every day like a rabid piñata. If I did my job right, Raymond would wake up and put on his papa pants. Even a hard-boiled elf like me can see if a kid has potential and, if his father gave half a damn, Little Ray had a chance of being a decent person. That was the plan.

At the Don't Hang Up headquarters, Raymond surrounded himself with a bunch of toothy cronies, grinning yes-men who knew a good seat on the gravy train when they saw one. Keeping the boss man happy kept their hands in the cookie jar, so several of them spent their entire days trying to think of a way to curry favor with the king. Years ago, one suck-up thought it might be clever to honor Raymond and his Don't Hang Up legacy with an old-fashioned telephone. He presented Raymond with a sleek, gleaming beauty with a rotary dial; it was as big as a boulder. Raymond loved it and rewarded the fellow with a promotion and a fat raise, so that started a tradition of who could find the boss other swell telephones. These eggs scoured flea markets and antiques shops across the globe coming up with every kind of ringer you could imagine—foreign jobs, spy phones, phone relics, the phones that belonged to gangsters and movie stars and stupid phones shaped like windmills and wiener dogs. Raymond loved them all and created a special room in his mansion for his collection. It was in that room that I would pay my own call to Raymond Hall.

None of the telephones were wired, but that's not a problem for an elf with a little magic up his sleeve. I slipped into Raymond's house about midnight and ambled into the phone room. Not a creature was stirring. The Halls were nestled all snug in their beds while visions that I didn't give a flip about danced in their heads.

Each phone stood like a statue in its own pool of light, and there must have been about fifty or sixty phones on shelves lining the walls. That made the middle of the room as dark as the inside of a cow, so that's where I took a chair and decided which telephone was going to ring first.

Raymond didn't exactly wake with a clatter. There was a cuckoo-clock phone on one of the higher shelves, so I threw a little elf spell its way. The bell was just barely a chirp, but then a little bird popped out. "Cuckoo-Cuckoo," it sang after each ring in a pitch not quite meant for any ear. In most of the homes in your world, I'm pretty sure this phone would have been the last noise someone heard before they started a killing spree with a dull ax. Next, I sent some hocus-pocus to a telephone that was as round as a stump with a ring like Judgment Day. It would rattle the teeth out of your head. Because something still seemed to be missing, and because I am a bitter stalk of rhubarb, I also got one more telephone going. This one replaced the ring with yodeling.

The room sounded like Lucifer's switchboard.

Raymond Hall entered the room half-asleep. The half that was awake had a "what the?" look that was taxing Raymond's medulla oblongata beyond its normal calculations. He turned his head between the different sounds as if they were trying to tell him something, but he didn't speak their lingo.

Ring-Cuckoo, Ring-Cuckoo!

RINGGGGGGGGGGGGGGGGG!

Odeleh-Hee-Whooo!

Standing there in his King Kong boxer shorts, cocking his head back and forth, Raymond looked like he had just escaped his rubber room. Finally, Raymond got his wits and decided he was mad at the stump telephone. Inspired by his underwear, Raymond took his mighty paw and swiped the contraption into the floor. The crash sounded like an accident at a munitions factory. Then, with the typical Raymond Hall temper, he grabbed the poker from the fireplace and started to beat the stump telephone like it had just soiled the rug.

I let Raymond think he killed the thing and stopped the ringer.

Ring-Cuckoo, Ring-Cuckoo!

Raymond threw the poker like a spear in the Bavarian phone's general direction, and, again, I shushed the bell.

Odeleh-Hee-Whooo!

"I hate yodeling!" Raymond screamed and threw the nearest knickknack at the telephone. There was a crash and then quiet except for Raymond's panting. Big boy needed to hit the gym.

"Knock knock," I said. I was still invisible.

Raymond jumped a mile. All the color drained from his face and his eyes were as big as canned hams. He searched the dark room in a panic, but he was too scared to move, a statue in King Kong bloomers.

"Knock knock," I said with a little bit of a growl.

"Who's there?" Raymond said. He wasn't playing around; he really wanted to know.

"Little old lady," I said.

"Huh?"

"I said, 'Knock knock,' you said, 'Who's there?' Little Old Lady. Now it's your turn," I explained.

Raymond took a step toward the direction of my voice, peering in the dark. "Little Old Lady Who?"

"I thought you said you hated yodeling," I said as I popped visible in front of him.

At the sudden sight of me, Raymond gripped his chest as all breath leaped from his lungs. He stared at me with an open mouth and eyes filled with terror. I smacked him across the face, hard, and sent him to the floor. "Take a picture. It'll last longer," I said.

Raymond spit out a tooth and a little blood. He looked like he was going to cry.

"It's not your night, Raymond Hall," I said. I turned a flip in the air, landed behind him and gave him a tough kick in the rump. Raymond went to his belly with a splat and a groan. "You've needed a good belting since you were a kid, so tonight you're going to take it and like it."

I picked Raymond up, spun him on his back and put a curled boot on his throat. He stared at me with bulging eyes, like I was a freight train with teeth. "Who are you?" he managed to gasp.

"Believe it or not, Ray, I'm one of Santa's elves," I said. Raymond curled his lip slightly, like he could feel a wave of bravery coming, so I gave that lip a kick just so Raymond would know that I wasn't trying to be cute. "You ready to listen?"

Raymond wasn't, but he jerked his head yes.

"Like I was saying, kid, I'm an elf and we help Santa

decide who's naughty and who's nice. All those lumps of coal you got over the years came from yours truly, but you never did learn, did you?" Raymond was speechless. "What did you do with the lumps of coal, Raymond?"

Raymond moved his lips to speak, but only managed a little croak, like a screen door. I had him on the ropes. For the first time in his life, he was scared.

"What did you do with the coal, Ray?"

"I don't remember!" he said just like any other guilty kid.

I gave him a kick in the King Kong. As he curled up into a little pathetic ball, I leaned in real close and screamed into his ear. "Wrong, Raymond! You do remember. One year, you threw the coal through the neighbor's living room window. The next year you picked off a bird's nest full of eggs. Another year, you bounced a coal rock off a little girl's head. She had to get stitches. Sixteen, if memory serves."

"Please!" Raymond said. He was drowning in Guilty River.

"You never learned your lesson, Raymond!"

"I was a kid," Raymond said. He was sobbing, the brat.

"That's no excuse," I said. "You're a big cheese now, and you're still breaking the rules, being bad. You still don't get it."

Scared and desperate, Raymond lost his head for a second, scrambled to his knees and took a wild swing at me. That was a mistake. I flew a telephone as solid as a bank safe right into Raymond's nose. "It's for you," I said.

Raymond crumpled to the ground in a heap. He was half-naked, bloodied and bruised, shamed to the bottom of the barrel. For a split second, I thought I went too far, but reminded myself that the beaten man in front of me could be Santa if greedy kids got their way.

"Dad?" It was Little Ray. He went white when he saw his father kiss the rug again. The kid looked at me like I was the boogeyman.

Raymond Senior managed to get up and put himself between me and the boy. "Son, get out of here!" Raymond screamed. "Call the cops!"

"No, Little Ray," I said. "I'm on my way out, but you need to hear this. Your dad's gonna tell you how important it is for you to be a good boy. To mind your mother and your teachers and be good to your friends. He's gonna teach you why it's important to think of others before yourself and to have a smile for someone, even strangers. You're gonna eat your peas and do your homework. Your dad will tell you why, right, Dad?"

"Yes, sure," Raymond said with a split lip. "I'll do whatever you ask, just don't hurt my son. Please, just go."

To make sure the lesson rang true, I cracked my knuckles and every telephone in the room, dozens of them, exploded into smithereens. When the echo of bells died away, Raymond had aged into a man, Little Ray had a chance at becoming something and I was feeling pretty full of myself. I mean, you know what they say: every time a bell rings, an angel gets his wings.

I walked to the window with a smile on my face, turned to Hall Senior and Junior and said, "Now be good for goodness' sake."

CHAPTER 8

Arose Such a Clatter

THE MARSHMALLOW WORLD GAZETTE

Cane Promises Elves Can Meet Toy Demand

An Exclusive Interview with Rosebud Jubilee

"It's not only beginning to look a lot like Christmas," one anonymous toy elf told me, "it's beginning to look like a chain gang. Santa is working everyone, including himself, to death. It takes some of the Holly Jolly out of it, you know?" Similar grumblings have been heard the past few weeks, but recently appointed toy czar Charles "Candy" Cane says rumors of overworked elves and Santa near exhaustion are "complete balderdash." Cane recently granted an exclusive powwow with yours truly. Here is a transcript of that interview.

Jubilee: So, Cane, what can you tell me about this charge of overworked elves?

Cane: Please call me Candy. I find it much sweeter, don't you?

Jubilee: How is Santa's health? The scuttle-butt is that you're working elves' fingers down to nubs. What gives?

Cane: Truth be told, elves' fingers are already nubs. That's a joke, Miss Jubilee, no reason to glower so! Although, I must say the fire in your eyes is positively radiant!

Jubilee: Listen, daisy, if you don't give me the square right now, I'm gonna use this pen to let a little daylight into that noodle of yours. Start jawing before you learn just how much mightier the pen is over the sword.

Cane: Business before pleasure, eh? Very well. Several weeks ago, I dismantled the entire Coal Patrol organization. I found the practices barbaric and without mercy, so I proposed to Santa that we concentrate on giving children, all children, something for Christmas, regardless of their be-havior. We feel that if children know they are loved, and these gifts are a reflection of love, they will behave accordingly.

Jubilee: But some elves think—

Cane: What I tell them to think, Miss Jubilee.

Jubilee: Aren't you putting a lot of extra work on Santa and the elves?

Cane: In the short term, yes, but actually, many of the elves are quite happy to work harder toward making this the best Christmas ever.

Jubilee: I hear Santa's losing weight. Why haven't we seen him?

Cane: Oh, he's quite busy. And I can assure you that the Fat Man's belly shakes like a bowl full of jelly.

Jubilee: What's Xanadu?

Cane: I happened to name the system that lets me review the quality of each toy after my estate.

Jubilee: Those reviews must keep you pretty busy.

Cane: I suppose, but I have a big appetite for work. I was thinking of buying *The Marshmallow World Gazette*. I think it would be fun to own a newspaper or two. Would you work for me, Miss Jubilee?

Jubilee: I don't think you'd like it. I bite.

Cane: I wouldn't mind that at all.

The article didn't bother me. Much. I was a little sore, though, about how Cane took a sledgehammer to the Coal Patrol I had built. I was sure he was telling a tall one about Santa's health, but I also knew there was nothing you were going to do to change St. Nick once his mind was made up. This new approach was just going to have to run its course and, in the end, Santa would decide if giving toys to every kid was right and fair. My mind was made up about that too. And I decided not to try and read between the lines on the subject of Cane and Rosebud. If she wanted to hang her stockings at Candy Cane manor, let her. What was it to me? Nothing, that's what.

In fact, the article didn't bother me as much as missing Dingleberry. After our pretend dustup a few days ago, we went our separate ways so he wouldn't get in Dutch with Cane. Plus, if Dingleberry knew what I had been up to, it would have broken his heart. In Ding's eyes, my behavior would be about as far from hero George as you could get, so I tried not to think about how much Dingleberry would hate my new job.

Instead, I tried to think on the good I was doing. After I fixed Raymond Hall's little red wagon, I turned invisible so I could hear what he said to Little Ray. Raymond took a giant step toward fatherhood. Not only did he give Little Ray a good talking-to that night, he followed up on it. Raymond made sure Little Ray minded, and was even trying to lead by example. Raymond was opening doors for old ladies, serving soup at the shelter and keeping his hands to himself. The boy noticed the change in his old man and was on the straight and narrow. My plan was working, so I got busy checking a few more off the Naughty Alumni List.

My next target was Octavia Dellora Mercedes Sprague. The stork did not deliver Octavia. I know the bird; he can spot bad news in the bundle before takeoff and would have given the job to a condor. When she arrived at the castle stoop, the silver spoon in Octavia's little mouth was already black with bile, gummed into an ugly wad of metal. Being born into high class was not enough for Octavia; she wanted more. She always wanted more and didn't care how many millions it cost Daddy.

Years ago, Octavia wanted a hippopotamus for Christmas. Only a hippopotamus would do. She stamped her feet, launched dishes at the help and put one butler in traction. At Coal Patrol, we said "no way" to Octavia's wish list and even Santa agreed. We delivered a bag of coal and Octavia took the lumps and broke out the stained glass windows of the cathedral—the one that her granddaddy had built.

With each Christmas, Octavia's demands became more and more outrageous. It was easier to know what she didn't want. And every year, we loaded her up with coal, but it didn't help. Christmas morning, Daddy would send some lackey on the hunt for whatever Octavia coveted. The hippo, by the way, was so miserable that he developed ulcers. He was dead by the Fourth of July and genuinely seemed glad to go.

Over the years, Octavia kept a parson and a divorce lawyer on retainer. Octavia Dellora Mercedes Sprague was now Octavia Dellora Mercedes Sprague-Cornwell-Lenox-Upglorious-Philadelphia (Octavia chose not to include "Pytingksy" on her list of husband hyphens because Itch was really just a fling, despite what the tattoo said). Most of the husbands discovered on the honeymoon that they were the *Titanic* and Octavia was the iceberg, but Lenox treaded water long enough to give Octavia a daughter.

Cordelia Heatherly Patricia Lenox couldn't have been less charming had she been made of pus. When it came to the brat torch, Cordelia took up where Mommy left off. Had it been an actual torch, I have no doubt the little lass would have used it to light cigars or orphanages.

After my elf magic conjured a hippo to chase Octavia around the golf course and shout her faults as a mother, little Cordelia turned into something close to a sweet little girl instead of the reason flamethrowers were invented.

It was good to love your work, but I wasn't done.

My next mission was Glen Page. Years ago, little Glen told Santa that all he wanted for Christmas was his two front teeth. We let him gnaw on a little coal instead because the truth was that Glen lost his two front choppers breaking into the school cafeteria to steal chocolate milk and meat loaf on a stick. Glen had not expected the shop teacher to be introducing the librarian to a little woodwork in the cafeteria freezer. When Glen opened the door, the surprised Mr. Cloniger grabbed a frozen meat loaf on a stick and clobbered Glen right in the mouth, sending his front teeth over the slaw.

At the North Pole, we thought Glen's dental gap and huge library fees would have taught him his lesson. The opposite was true. Glen became a Peeping Tom and was raising Glen Junior, a child who would only inspire happiness in others if he was playing with a grenade and the pin was pulled.

To help Glen change his ways and inspire his kid to do the same, I cornered Glen outside the window of a sorority house and flossed the old man with a ball bat.

I was making progress. Kids and parents were getting the message. It was easy.

It was too easy.

I didn't think anyone would figure it out.

But somebody snitched on me.

CHAPTER 9

Stink, Stank, Stunk

I almost didn't hear the knock at the door, the tapping was so quiet. The hour was late and I wasn't expecting company. I hadn't been around anyone except the human parents I was slapping around, so I went to the door hoping for some Holly Jolly elf companionship. When I opened the door, what I saw shook me right down to my socks.

Santa looked like he was made of rope, he was so skinny and gangly. The Fat Man was spread thin. The big belly, the rosy cheeks, the twinkle in his eyes—they were all gone. In their place was a stick bum in a baggy red suit. Santa's lush white beard was coming out in mangy clumps and his hair was flat and slick. Worst of all, you could tell Santa had been crying.

Santa stared at me for a good half a minute with those sad, tired eyes before he said in a hoarse whisper, "May I come in, Gumdrop?"

I lost my voice, but I managed to swing the door open and show him to the couch. He rested there for a minute and then noticed all the questions in my eyes. "Sit down, son," he said. "Sit down."

"You don't look so good, Nick," I said, pulling up a chair.

"Good," he said with a slight smile. "I don't feel so well either, my boy, so I am glad that I am not mismatched."

"You're working too hard, Santa."

"You are probably right, Gumdrop," Santa said. "But the work of giving is not what is troubling me. How have you been spending your time recently, son?" Suddenly, Santa's jaw was tight, his eyes still. He was steeling himself for the lie he knew I was going to tell him.

"I've been keeping myself occupied," I said, getting as close to the truth as was comfortable for the moment. "I've traveled some. I'm just trying to figure what to do next."

It wasn't the answer Santa wanted to hear, so he turned his head away like he didn't want to look at me when he called me on the carpet. "I know you've been traveling," he said. "And I am heartbroken at how you've been keeping yourself occupied."

I couldn't lie to the old man. "How'd you find out?"

"Shame on you!" Santa said in the coldest voice I'd ever heard. "Shame on you! An elf represents the North Pole, Gumdrop, just as much as I do. You physically assaulted people, embarrassed them, frightened them. You frightened children, Gumdrop!"

"I went after the parents, Nick," I said.

"Well, little Raymond Hall Junior wrote me a letter and told me that an elf, one of my elves, beat up his father with a telephone," Santa thundered back. "The child saw it; he was there. I can only imagine what that little, little boy will think of the Christmas season for the rest of his life."

"I hope he will see the season for what it's supposed to be," I said. "A time for thinking about somebody other than yourself."

"Pity you could not heed that same advice," Santa said. "I now know this is not about keeping children from becoming naughty; it's not about the integrity of Christmas or even a dose of tough love. This is Gumdrop Coal's personal vendetta and it saddens me to the bottom of my heart."

"You're wrong, Santa," I said. "I can see why it looks that way, but you're wrong."

Santa seemed surprised at my tone. After a moment, he shook his head and said. "I'm sorry, but I don't believe you."

"Then you're listening too much to Candy Cane," I

said. I was getting angry. "He's been spreading whoppers about me since before all this started."

"Are you honestly trying to blame your behavior on Candy?" Santa asked. "Did he attack those children's parents? Did he make a child afraid at Christmastime? I suppose you agree with your little Misfit friend, Sherlock Stetson, that Candy also heads up the Misfit Mafia."

"I don't know anything about that, Santa," I said. "All I know is that once Citizen Cane burst onto the scene, you started giving me and my work the stink eye. Before I know it, I'm out, he's in and every brat with a wish is getting what it wants for Christmas. It doesn't seem fair and there seems to be more to it than that, but I don't know what. You don't look so good, Nick. Maybe Sherlock is on to something after all. Weren't there threats after Mr. Snowman was plowed over?"

Santa held up his hand; he had heard enough. He got to his feet and walked to the door without looking back. He opened the door and paused. "Promise me you will leave humans alone. All humans. Children and parents."

"They need discipline, Santa," I said. "Things need to be just. Their wants will kill you."

"Promise me. If you are harming anyone, I don't know if I would have the heart to be a part of Christmas anymore. Promise me, Gumdrop," he said with his back to me.

If I said "no," Christmas was off. If I said "yes," there

was a good chance Santa wouldn't make it through Christmas. I didn't like my spot, but I knew I wouldn't be able to stand the look in Santa's eyes if I didn't do what he asked. "I promise," I said.

Santa left without another word.

I never felt so ashamed in my life.

That is until Dingleberry arrived at my door a few minutes later. He didn't speak; he sobbed. I poured him a stiff eggnog and let him blubber a few minutes to see if it would get out of his system. I didn't say anything. I was afraid I'd make it worse—or start blubbering myself.

Finally, Dingleberry blew his schnoz and took a deep breath. "I guess by the look on your face, what I heard is true," he said.

"I'm sorry to say that it is."

"Oh, Gumdrop, you did a bad thing," Dingleberry said. "A bad, bad thing. You *hurt* people. You used your gift of elf magic to go into people's homes and hit them and scream at them."

"It is not as simple as that," I said. "And you know why I did it."

"Yeah, because you *hate* the naughty!" he screamed. "You *hate* anyone who doesn't do things the way you think they should be done."

"Cane put that idea in your head?" I asked. I could tell by Dingleberry's expression that I was right. "Dingleberry, you know, deep down, that is not true. You know I *hate* naughtiness. I hate when kids take Santa for granted. I hate that parents don't teach their kids any better. You know I'm trying to help them, or you did know that. I guess Cane has changed your mind. Some friend you are."

It was a lousy thing to say, but I was feeling like everyone was piling on. Why didn't anyone understand?

Dingleberry was wounded, but he held it together. Shaking, he stood up and looked me right in the eye. "Maybe you're right. Maybe I'm not a good friend to you. But I am a good elf, Gumdrop, a good elf. I am here to make toys for children, to make them happy whether they're good or bad. It's what George would do too. He knows what is right and so do I."

"This isn't one of your stupid comic book yarns," I said. I was starting to lose my famous temper. "This is real stuff, Ding. You can't let bad kids and awful parents slide on a lifetime of naughty. The folks on the Nice List would have no reason to be nice. That's not fair. And it's not fair that everyone's kicking me in the pants over this. Why beat me up when you won't punish a brat? If I were a kid out in the real world, you'd be building me some lamebrain *By George* adventure set and giving it to me Christmas morning with no questions asked!"

Dingleberry was shot through the heart, but he

didn't fall like a ton of bricks. He got up and went to the door. "That's different. They're kids, Gumdrop. I'm sorry if that seems unfair to you, but it's all I know," he said. "So because it's all I know, I don't think I can be your best friend. And *By George* is not fake, and he's not stupid. He doesn't make people do things his way. He doesn't slap them around and snap their head off. He does things the right way and inspires everybody else to do things the right way too. 'Treat the other guy like you were in his boots.' That's part of the *By George True Friends* pledge. I'm trying to do that, Gumdrop, but right now, I don't want to be in your boots because all you want to do in them is walk all over people."

And then Dingleberry left. I called after him, but he kept going.

I know the song says not to pout, not to cry. But under the circumstances, I figured I was entitled. I sat in the dark all through the wee hours trying to untie my knot of trouble, wondering if it could get any worse. I drank more than a little cheer to help me think. Instead, I forgot. And slept. A few groggy hours later, I was about to take a little satisfaction thinking I was at rock bottom. Then, there was a knock at the door.

It got worse all right. Brother, did it get worse.

CHAPTER 10

Decorations of Red

Dear Gumdrop,

The game's afoot! I have deduced that there really is a Misfit Mafia! Great Caesar's Ghost! I may need your help, so stay close!

Sherlock Stetson

P.S. Zsa Zsa says hello to her vittle Gumdrop and that if you've got the chimney sweeper, she's got the flue. Don't worry; I'll get her some soup.

When I opened my door, I saw Bert the Cop on my welcome mat, looking like dinner hadn't agreed with him for the past ten years. I made it my business to look hard and see if there was a firing squad behind him, so I didn't notice the note from Sherlock sticking

82

out of my mailbox by the door. If I had, the rest of my night might have turned out a lot different. But I didn't and it was time to tuck into the bed I had made.

A cop was the last thing I needed, but my guess was that my little jaunts into the human world had broken some ancient Kringle Town law. I figured Santa had sent Bert to write me a ticket or, at least, give me a warning. I might even get a couple of days in the hoosegow to cool off, but I was past caring. I swung the door open and motioned Bert in, just to get it over with.

"Holly Jolly, Bert," I said, pointing to a chair. "You're a little far from home. How are things in Bedford Falls?"

"It's a wonderful life there," Bert said. He sat, but he wasn't comfortable. He was checking out my place as quickly as he could with a glance. He frowned when what he was looking for didn't show up. "How have you been, Gumdrop? I hear you've had a little trouble lately."

"Well, I caused most of it, and Santa's already read me the riot act," I said. "If he sent you to rap my knuckles or throw me in the pokey to teach me a lesson, I'll play nice, Bert. I'm done being a tough elf."

"Santa didn't send me, Gum," Bert said. "I'm here on kind of official business. Where have you been in the last twelve hours or so?"

"Right here."

"Alone, I suppose."

"Santa was here about 7:30," I said. "Dingleberry was right behind him. I started keeping company with a bottle of cheer from about 8:30 on."

"That was eight hours ago," Bert said, frowning.

"I wasn't awake for all of them, so I'll trust your math," I said. "Tell me, Bert, what do you think I might have been up to in those eight hours?"

Bert stared at me level, cold. "Raymond Hall Senior is dead," he said like he hated saying it. "His kid found him. Human cops figure he had only been dead a couple of hours." Bert pulled a notepad and a pen out of his pocket and flipped to a blank page. "Know anything about it?"

I waited for a few seconds before I tried to come up with an answer that would make Bert close his pad. I was hoping it was some kind of gag, but the ice in Bert's eyes told me all I needed to know. I returned Bert's stare and said, "No, Bert. I don't know anything. I haven't seen Hall since I roughed him up last week. Hadn't even thought about him until Santa came in and took me behind the woodshed. I know it looks bad, but that's the truth."

Bert gave the inside of his cheek a chew and then scribbled a note. "You'll get a fair shake from me, Gumdrop, you know that," he said. "But don't think I'll play the sap for you. If you did this, even Clarence the angel won't be able to save you."

"What happened?" I asked.

According to what Bert heard through the grapevine, Little Ray found his dad in the telephone room. Senior was on the floor, beat up, blood everywhere. The kid called the cops and they had been taking pictures and dusting ever since. Bert heard that the human cops were stumped because there was no sign of a break-in, no weapon and no one else in the house.

"So naturally you think an elf with magical powers got in, whacked Raymond and got out," I said. "That would explain why the human cops are stymied."

"It would explain a lot of things," Bert said.

"Have you gone to Hall's house?" I asked.

"Wanted to come here first," Bert said. "I wanted to see if you were here and how you would take the news."

"How'd I do?"

"So far, you're a cool customer, I'll give you that," Bert said. He scanned my place again, studying.

"Looking for a murder weapon?"

"You got a typewriter, Gumdrop?"

"You think I gave Raymond Hall the powder with a typewriter, Bert?"

Bert gave me a hard look and then fished a piece of paper out of his pocket and handed it to me. "Someone sent this to *The Marshmallow World* earlier tonight. Know anything about it?"

I took the paper and read it. Somebody was writing me a death sentence and they did it on a typewriter.

'Twas the night before Christmas, when all through the
   home,

The Creature stirred trouble, wherever he roamed;

The kittens were hung by the chimney with glee,

By a miserable kid who was really naughty;

The brat was nestled, cold-blooded in bed,

While visions of misery danced in his head;

And Momma drinking bourbon, and I with my pills,

Hid from our child that we wanted to kill;

When out on the lawn there arose such a clatter,

I sprang from my bed to see what was the matter;

It sounded like the kid emptied a drawer full of knives;

I peeked out the door, afraid for our lives;

When what to my wondering eyes should appear,

But an elf famous for giving kicks in the rear;

He had rocks on his back and soot in his soul,

I knew in an instant he was Gumdrop Coal.

"Now hellion, now rascal, now little brat!

"This is what you get for being a rat!"

He spoke not a word, but went straight to his work,

Giving coal to my kid, the little jerk;

With a snarl, Gumdrop bit the Gingerbread Man's head,

Spit out the crumbs and left the ginger carcass for dead;

And I heard him exclaim as left in a bound,

"Say so long to the Fat Man, there's a new elf in town!"

I could feel Bert staring hard at me while I read. I was in a tough spot. "I don't really think 'naughty' and 'glee' rhyme, do you?" I asked, handing the paper back.

"Trying to be cute, huh?" Bert asked. "Your mug shot's not going to be so cute, wise guy."

"Smart up, Bert," I said. "Somebody's putting the shuck on me and you. This little limerick just happens to show up the night Raymond Hall is mysteriously rubbed out and you don't think that's fishy? You believe that I wrote it after I killed Raymond and sent it in just for kicks? Next you'll tell me you believe in the Tooth Fairy."

"Watch your mouth or you'll be missing a few teeth," Bert said, meaning it.

"C'mon, Bert. Someone's playing you."

"I don't play at being a cop," Bert said. "You're the number one suspect, until I think different. But like I said, I'm giving you a fair shake."

"I appreciate it," I said. I gave us half a minute to cool down and then asked, "Do you think I could tag along with you to see Raymond?"

"Sounds like you want to return to the scene of the crime," Bert said, getting up.

"I want to be there when you investigate," I said. "I want to clear my name of this tonight."

hen Bert and I arrived at the Hall house, the human cops were still there. We stood silent and invisible on the border of Kringle Town and the human world, watching them do their grim work. Bert took notes on his pad and I tried to ignore the wails of sorrow coming from the other side of the house. It was a tough break that Little Ray found his dad. He probably hated my guts. I would if I were in his shoes. His dad was a mess. There was more blood than I was expecting; his face was decorated in red. Just looking at it made my stomach churn, but I was pretty sure upchucking would make me look even more guilty—not that I needed any help.

On the human side, a big detective came in with a medical examiner and cleared the room. "I want to see if you can tell me how this guy died before I mess with the crime scene any more," the detective told the doctor. "We can't find a single print, a broken window or door, nothing. We can't find a weapon, so see if you can give me any idea of what else to look for."

The doctor opened his sack and began looking for his tools. The big detective stepped back and waited, studying the room for anything he might have missed.

Somewhere far behind Bert and me there was a noise, a kind of dull rumble. It was coming from Kringle

Town and headed our way. As it got closer, we could make out that it was the voices of elves. They were shouting my name. They were mad. They were coming after me.

The one voice rising over the throng, the angriest, the one leading the pack, belonged to Kringle Town's rising citizen—Cane.

"You can arrest me, Bert," I said. "But you got to keep that mob from tearing me apart."

"Don't move," Bert growled and stomped off toward the crowd. I watched him go and wondered if it made more sense for me to run. On the one hand, it would prove to every elf in Kringle Town that I was as guilty as I could be. On the other hand, it sounded like most of the elves didn't need any help with that idea. I was trying to figure how I could build my defense when the medical examiner called the detective over to Raymond's body.

"You might want to check around for bullet holes again, Detective," the doctor said, shining a light at Raymond's bloody head. "I was trying to find where all this blood came from, but I couldn't find a wound and then I caught the reflection of something."

"What is it?" the detective asked, peering in. Invisible to the human cops, I peered in too.

The doctor worked a pair of tiny tweezers just above Raymond's right cheek. Slowly, the doctor pulled

something out. "This," he said, holding the tiny object up to the detective. "It's a BB. Someone shot his eye out."

My neck went clammy and I got dizzy as a top. Whoever knocked off Raymond Senior went to a great deal of trouble to hide how they did it. Something told me that I was getting railroaded and that whoever was driving the train was in that mob and coming up fast. I wasn't going to have time to explain everything so we could find out who did this to Raymond. I wasn't going to have time to go to Raymond Junior and tell him I was sorry and that he and his dad didn't deserve this. The only way to get more time was to run no matter how guilty it made me look. I needed to figure out the who and the why. My bright idea opened the door for someone to kill Raymond, but I didn't have to let them get away with it.

I owed it to Raymond and Little Ray.

I owed it to Santa.

I owed it to every kid who wanted to believe in something good.

I had one clue: an eye shot out with a BB.

Ralphie!

CHAPTER 11

Over the River and Through the Woods

THE MARSHMALLOW WORLD GAZETTE

Elf Collector Scores Rare Comic

Talk to Dingleberry Fizz for more than a minute and you'll discover two things he loves: making toys and *By George Adventures*. Kringle Comics has been publishing the plucky yarns of Bedford Falls' most famous lassoer for decades, creating one of comics' most enduring characters. But to fans like Dingleberry Fizz, *By George* is a guide to life. "He is just the best," Dingleberry gushes. "He's brave, he's funny, he's smart. He's a dreamer and he always finds a way to make his dream come true—even if he's running from a tribe of Mayan Piggy Pygmies through a maze of mutant okra plants. He did that too, you know." Because others share Fizz's hero worship of *By George Adventures*, many of the early comics are hard to come by and can cost a pretty penny. But Dingleberry Fizz recently had a stroke of luck on Elf-Bay. "Someone was getting rid of their older brother's comic book collection. He had a lot of *By George Adventures*, so I bought them for spares. I never, ever thought I'd find issue 48, but it was mixed in with all the rest. It's worth more than what I paid for the whole collection!" Issue 48 is the *By George Adventures* holy grail, a rare, hard-to-find potboiler, *The Disappearing Rabbit*. In *The Disappearing Rabbit*, George rescues the daughter of a gazillionaire who has been kidnapped by an evil magician. In rescuing the lass, George gets unexpected help from the magician's loyal rabbit, Harvey. Written and illustrated by the famous artist Robert May, *The Disappearing Rabbit* was a single-issue adventure. The limited printing makes the issue even more valuable. Experts estimate that, in mint condition, *The Disappearing Rabbit* could be worth as much as six hundred sugarplums. Knowing that, Fizz simply quotes his hero, "Hot dog!"

f Dingleberry's comic score was the big news, then the papers had not yet learned of my outlaw ways. I imagine Rosebud was sharpening her poison pen, and a special edition was rolling off the presses, lots of ink and hard words telling of the awful thing I had done. But for the moment, I was still free. I had a chance to change how the story ended.

As soon as I heard that a BB to the eye is what put Raymond under the white sheet, I had a hunch that I was being framed. Someone from Kringle Town knew I had roughed up Raymond. They also knew that I would be the prime suspect if something happened to him. Even if Bert had heard the examiner say that someone had shot Raymond's eye out, he and every other Kringle Town citizen would have said that I chose the whole BB angle as a cover.

So I ran.

I figured running was the only chance I had. It was the only way I could find out if Ralphie had his hands on the trigger of an Official Red Ryder Carbine-Action Two-Hundred-Shot Range Model BB Gun with a compass in the stock. It didn't sound like something Ralphie would do. Ralphie was a good kid, a bit of a potty mouth, but a good kid. Either someone *made* Ralphie shoot Raymond, or Ralphie was another fall guy. Either way, I had to get to Ralphie before anyone else did and make sure he would tell the truth.

I ducked into the human world and hid in a tree outside the Hall house. When Bert arrived with Cane's posse and saw me gone, they took off the way they came. They thought I doubled back on them and stampeded away to cut me off. I let them get good and gone while I watched the cops take Raymond's body away. Raymond was a rotten kid and not much of a dad until the end, but I still didn't want to see him dead. A prayer for Raymond hung in a lump in my throat for a while, not because I didn't think he deserved one. I just wasn't sure I deserved to pray it.

When it was safe, I jumped back into Kringle Town and headed for Ralphie. Though he was always going to be around eleven years old, more or less, Ralphie was wise beyond his years. Behind the big round glasses was a guy who knew something about the heartbreak of wanting something so bad you could taste it. He also knew that once you got it, the thing that you wanted wasn't what was missing in the first place. That's what Ralphie's job was in Kringle Town, to remind us all to look beyond what we crave and take joy in what we have.

Still, Ralphie was a kid and I suppose that if someone made using Raymond Hall for target practice sound like an adventure, Ralphie might have gone along with the idea. There was only one way to find out, so I knocked on Ralphie's door.

It was late and the dull glow of the leg lamp in the window didn't do much to cut the gloom. The house was as dark as a bat's gut. My knock was the only sound and nobody was stirring inside. Since Bert, Cane and the mob could be on me in a matter of minutes, I decided to forget my manners and let myself in. Actually, I just walked through the door. Elf magic comes in handy.

The place was a mess. Dishes with half-eaten meals covered most of the flat surfaces in the front room by the radio and the floor was a carpet of newspapers, clothes and crumbs. Propped up in the corner was Ralphie's prized Red Ryder Carbine-Action Two-Hundred-Shot Range Model BB Gun with a compass in the stock. Its dark barrel winked in the low light, which meant it had just been cleaned. I hoisted it up and was giving it the once-over, looking for any kind of clue, when Ralphie scampered down the stairs in a hurry. He stopped in his tracks when he saw me, went pale and threw his hands above his head.

"Relax, Ralphie," I told him. "You're not being robbed." Though I must admit that I kept the Red Ryder aimed just above Ralphie's head.

"Gumdrop," the kid managed to get out between the thumping of his heart. "What are you doing here?"

"Just dropping in on an old pal," I said. "You seem kind of surprised to see me, kid. Why is that?"

"I wasn't expecting to run into someone pointing a gun at me," he said. "What's so strange about that?"

"Nothing, I guess. Why don't you relax? I just need to ask you a couple of questions."

Ralphie didn't budge. His arms were still frozen above his head. "I can't put my arms down," he said. "I'm scared."

Feeling ashamed, I lowered the gun. Even if Ralphie was guilty, I had no business pointing a rifle at a kid. "Easy, buddy," I said. "I was just looking at your rifle. Sit down. Do you know why I'm here?"

Without taking his eyes off me, Ralphie found a chair. He sat quiet for a minute and then tears started to well up behind those big round glasses. "I heard on the radio that you did something bad, Gumdrop," he blubbered. "You killed that man. You tricked me into giving you my BB gun and you killed him! And now you're going to say it was me who did it and it wasn't! It wasn't me!"

The kid was out of control now. He was sobbing and shaking. Tears poured out of his eyes, and his nose was Niagara Falls. I had to get him calmed down before he started losing his dinner. I sat down beside him and gave him a hankie. I patted him on the back and tried to stay calm despite knowing that something was going on in Kringle Town and that I was in the middle of it.

"Calm down, kid," I said. "Calm down. I know you didn't do it and I'm not here to make you take the blame." Ralphie eased off the sobbing throttle a bit, so I plowed on. "I didn't kill Raymond Hall. I hurt him last week, but he was alive. Whoever killed him tonight wants it to look like I did it and I need your help to find out who it is. Do you think you can help me?"

My hankie would have been drier if it had come out of the ocean. After Ralphie got finished filling it with his sinuses, he seemed a little less unhinged. I needed to get answers out of him in a hurry, but I didn't want to set him off again. "Let's start at the beginning, kid," I told him. "What makes you think I tricked you into giving me your BB gun?"

"You sent me a note saying that you wanted to borrow it," he said. "You said that if I let you borrow it, you would give me what I really wanted."

"What's that?"

"To grow up." Ralphie's face started to melt into tears again. "I'm tired of being a kid! I want to grow up and do other things. I want to get tall and finally outgrow that stupid, dupid bunny suit! I want a red car. I want a mustache! You said you could make it happen if I let you borrow Red Ryder!"

Poor kid. I guess Ralphie's mission in life was getting to him and he wasn't happy with what he had. Most of us in Kringle Town are content to stay more or less the same, so you folks in the human world can have your holiday traditions. Oh sure, along about July, everybody gets a little itch to break out of the mold, but most of us are happy to do our jobs. Ralphie was having a hard time adjusting. He has to stay the same soap-eating, theme-writing, bunny-suit-wearing boy forever—and that was no picnic. "Ralphie, were the notes signed by me?" I asked.

Ralphie pinched up his face in hard thought and then shook his head. "No. After I heard the news tonight, I just thought the note was from you." Ralphie fished a piece of paper out of his pocket and handed it to me.

Dear Ralphie,

    I need your help to play a trick on someone. Cupid over in Valentine Town has challenged me to a target contest. He thinks he is going to win because he is so good with that bow and arrow. But here's the thing: Cupid never said that I had to use a bow and arrow! Now everyone knows that the Official Red Ryder Carbine-Action Two-Hundred-Shot Range Model BB Gun with a compass in the stock turns anyone into a real marksman, so I was wondering if I could borrow "Old Blue" to put that diaper-wearing matchmaker in his place? I'll make it worth your while. I believe I can arrange for your secret wish to be granted.

You will get to grow up! This must all be kept
secret, though, until after the contest.
Please help me, Ralphie. Please deliver Red
Ryder to P.O. Box U-Who by Tuesday.

>   Sincerely,
>   A Friend

The note was written with a typewriter and could
have come from anybody. The P.O. Box was an address
in Whoville. "Did you see anybody when you delivered
the gun?" I asked Ralphie.

"I didn't go at first," he said. "As much as I want to
grow up, I didn't want anyone to have my Red Ryder. I
worked hard for it."

"What changed your mind?"

Ralphie pulled out a second scrap of paper and
handed it to me.

Dear Ralphie,
    Since you failed to deliver the Red Ryder to
me, I am forced to resort to baser tactics.
Ralphie, deliver the Red Ryder to me
tomorrow--I DOUBLE DOG DARE YOU!

Now that was an offer Ralphie couldn't refuse.

"I took it this morning," Ralphie said. "Someone left
Red Ryder on the porch a few hours ago. I never saw who."

I scrambled to try and put the millions of puzzle pieces in my mind together, but I couldn't find a single match. The only thing I had to go on was that the Red Ryder was delivered to Whoville, a burg of Kringle Town that asks more questions than it answers, so folks don't tend to go there unless they absolutely have to. Still, I had to find out who was behind all of this.

Or which Who.

I got all the details about Ralphie's trip to Whoville and I slipped the notes in my pocket. "Now, Ralphie, remember this," I said. "You never saw me; we never talked. Until I figure out a few things, you keep your trap shut and don't tell anyone about someone borrowing Red Ryder."

"But," Ralphie said, looking scared. I imagine the kid didn't want to have to lie anymore.

"No buts," I said, cutting him off. "You can't talk. I triple dog dare you."

I headed for Whoville in a hurry, though I was dreading it. I don't like the town. They got their own way of running things and if you don't play by their rules, you stick out in Whoville like I don't know what. You'll see. But I didn't have a choice. My trail would stay cold a few minutes more, but then Bert, Cane and the mob would be hot on my trail quicker than a dime store Santa in a greased chimney.

CHAPTER 12

Seasick Crocodile

Every Who
Down in Whoville
Liked mysteries a lot

They liked Whodunits
With puzzles and riddles,
Cases with knots in the plot.

A Who brain could help me. Find who
borrowed the gun.
A Who'd study the clues, think it was fun.
It could be the killer's head wasn't
screwed on quite right.
It could be, perhaps, it just wasn't my night.
I had to find for whom I was taking the fall.
Else, I'd get fitted for a noose, two sizes too small.

But,

Ukulele Who,

Known as U. Who,

Was an old friend and he'd know what to do.

He had eyes in the alleys, ears to the ground.

If crime stank just a little, he had the nose of a hound.

So I snuck to his door, gave it a rap,

Looking over my shoulder, hoping it wasn't a trap.

"Gumdrop, you've got some nerve," U. Who said.

"You're hot as a pepper! Could get us all dead!"

"Then you know the lowdown on the rifle," I begged.

"Tell me what you know, friend, then I promise I'll leg."

"Someone rented a Who mailbox.

They got Ralphie's Red Ryder.

They're spinning a web

And I want the spider!"

U. Who thought

Hard about what I asked.

Then he kicked the door. "Blast!"

He shouted and steamed. "Blast, blast, blast, blast!"

U. Who said, "Lou Who gave his box to

Some femme fatale.

Lou Who got to first base, but now don't feel so well.

What she did to him, she should be ashamed!
Lou's in a sugar coma from too much candy cane!"

I wanted to cry, but it wasn't my style.
I felt worse than a seasick crocodile.
It was one thing for Cane to want me dead,
But was he getting help from the dame
named for a sled?

Then U. Who handed me a note.
A dilly of a note.
U. Who
Gave me a real dilly of a note.

"This paper got here just before you,
Like they knew you were coming. It smells of perfume."
I could not believe the words that I read
But the quick little letter filled me with dread.

"Run your pucker to the Forest of Mistletoe!
Shut up! Now! Go! Put your lips together and blow!"

CHAPTER 13

Somebody Waits for You

THE MARSHMALLOW WORLD GAZETTE

Do You Hear What I Hear?

Gossip with Butternut Snitch

The grapevine is ripe with rumors of elf-in-exile Gumdrop Coal's whereabouts. Talk around the eggnog-cooler is that the outlaw elf is behind Kringle Town's new crime spree. Some rubber-neckers claim that they saw "Gumdrop-Dead" snatch a purse from the bishop's wife, and others said Coal gave some nosy sugarplums double vision. Since there are rumors that the "Ghost of Christmas Panic" is planning more trouble, Candy Cane has convinced Santa to give the Tin

Soldiers marching orders. Speaking of Kringle Town's eye Candy, no one has heard "boo" from scoop siren Rosebud Jubliee. Honchos say she is covering the Gumdrop elf-hunt from the field, but I have also heard that someone has pulled some Xanadu voodoo to hide Jubliee's button from danger. *Is the love light beaming? Stay tuned!*

*T*he road to the Forest of Mistletoe was as bleak as prom time for the homely. I kept to the shadows and alleys, read news out of trash bins and pinched a bite to eat from the scraps wrapped in the headlines that were calling for my head. So far, they were still looking for me in Kringle Town proper, but I was pretty sure that was Cane's doing. He was setting me up to take the fall for Raymond's murder and the girl who knew how to tell a story was in on the fix. If Cane were trying to put the Fat Man on a permanent diet, he'd need help and I suppose he offered to buy Rosebud a newspaper to play with. So she trots her cute little self to Whoville, gives Lou Who the come-hither for his mailbox. They get the Red Ryder, kibosh Raymond, give Lou the sweet sayonara and the trail is colder than a North Pole outhouse. What they don't count on is that I'm on to them, so they leave the little note to meet them in the woods where there would be nobody around. Pretty nifty. If I went to Bert or Santa with this story, I'd sound guilty and like I was the top nut on the fruitcake. They only choice I had was to take the bait and see if I could wiggle off the hook later.

The Forest of Mistletoe was the perfect place to tuck someone in for the big sleep. Lost in all the pucker talk, mistletoe is sometimes called the "vampire" plant because that's what it is. Mistletoe attaches itself to a tree or shrub and sucks the life out of it. Think about that the next time some cute tomato gives you the come-hither standing under the twig. In the Forest of Mistletoe, the botany isn't satisfied simply dining on trees. It wants blood and is partial to the sweet life-smack that pumps through elf veins. Many a short-round has gone into the Forest of Mistletoe on a dare, but none has ever come back. You might find an elf carcass, shriveled like a popped pimple, lying at the edge of the forest, but that was about it. There were crazy tales that some didn't die but survived as some kind of mutant vampire elf. Rural and conspiracy elves claimed to have seen little monster dwarfs tearing through the bracken, thirsty for fresh blood. There was also talk that roving bands of elf vamps swooped down on the Isle of Misfit Toys on dark and haunted nights and feasted on the forgotten playthings. The tales sounded like something from Dingleberry's *By George Adventures*, so I didn't believe any of it. But when you stood in front of a wall of trees that was as dark as the inside of a chimney with the damper closed, it did take some of the starch out of your tights.

There was a sad excuse for a trail leading into the woods and I'm not too proud to admit that I took my time hiking it. The gloom that rose up before me was about as comforting as hearing a bump under the bed. A wicked wind trolled through the dark air, making the hard old trees creak like the coffins of residents who forgot they were dead. I wasn't anxious to go skipping in there, especially knowing someone was laying a trap for me, so I was glad to be distracted by the three French hens.

"Bonjour," said one.

"Bonjour," said another.

"Hiya, mac," said the third.

I came up on them as I rounded a bend just before I went into the Forest of Mistletoe for good. They were sitting on a rock, surrounded by the remains of a picnic. Their feathers were puffed up to keep the cold out and all three were getting help with little capes that were draped over their tails. The two hens on the left were identical, white and real lookers. As I got closer, I could see that the third hen was clearly a duck. And a guy duck. He looked like he had just survived getting plucked by a blind man, but barely.

Since they were French, I gave them a deep bow and said, "Whose acquaintance do I have the pleasure of making?"

"Oh, I am Coco," said the first, giggling.

"I am Luci," said the second. She blushed three shades of red.

"I'm Fuzz," said the duck with a burp. "We ate all the food. If you're beggin', keep hiking, piker."

I gave Fuzz a tough gander. "Relax, Fuzz," I said. "I'm well-chowed and I don't go for chicken feed. Speaking of which, you are clearly not of the same feather as these ladies. What gives?"

"Oh, Antoinette," squeaked Coco.

"Au revoir," Luci said with a tear in her eye.

"Apparently, their big sister amscrayed," Fuzz said. "They said she ran off with some colonel guy who promised her a bucket of fun."

"Sounds like Antoinette lost her head," I said.

"C'est la vie," Fuzz said. "It's like water off of my back."

"And you're here to give them a shoulder to cry on," I said, sizing Fuzz up in a second.

"*Oui!*" Coco cooed.

"*Oui!*" Luci chirped.

"Hey, I don't claim to be no Don Swan," Fuzz said, getting a little ruffled. "But they are cute chicks and they are *French*. Do I have to draw you a picture?"

"No thanks," I said. "I'll wait and catch it on the late late show. How long have birds been hanging around here?"

"A couple of days," Fuzz said. "It's nice and quiet up here. You don't get a lot of Nosey Parkers minding your beeswax in this neck of the woods. Good for the amour, you know?"

"*Oui, oui*," Coco and Luci said with a kind of enthusiasm that would turn you off eggs for good.

"Seen anybody go into the forest?" I asked.

Fuzz gave me the once-over and, for a minute, I was afraid he had been reading the news and caught on as to who I was. But it ended up that Fuzz was just worried how much longer this chitchat was going to go on before he could return to getting henpecked. "There was another elf a couple of days ago," he said, pointing his beak toward the trail. "He didn't stop to talk. Seemed like he was in a hurry to move along. He didn't look like he was made out for the outdoorsy stuff, though. He was a real dandy."

"Well, Candy is dandy," I said mostly to myself.

"What's that, buster?" Fuzz asked. "I didn't catch that."

"Nothing, Fuzz. Anybody with this elf?"

"Yeah, some doll," Fuzz said with a dirty grin. "I think that's why he was in a hurry. Do I have to draw you a picture?"

Fuzz didn't have to draw me a picture. The picture I had hit me in the gut like a jackhammer. *She* was with him, helping him. Of course, that poem that came to the paper was written *at* the paper, on her own little

Royal typewriter. I was a schmuck. I tried to give myself a kick and tell my heart that it didn't matter. I wasn't really the type for whispering sweet nothings and slow dances. I wasn't known for moonlight and mush. I've never dotted an "I" with a heart or lingered in the shadows saying "night-night" a million times. I told myself that the lump in my throat would pass probably about the time I got my third set of teeth. "What did this doll look like?" I asked it like I didn't care, but the effort was like trying to do push-ups with an elephant on your back.

"She was cute," Fuzz said with a shrug. "I didn't really get a good look at her, because she really isn't my type. I mean, I wouldn't go *a l'orange* for her, but I could see why some guys would. The dandy followed her like a baby duck."

"Thanks," I said, though I would have preferred it if he had put a pipe through my skull. "I'm heading into the woods, but I'll make sure I steer clear of them. I don't want to disturb their amore."

"That's a rough patch of thatch in there, buster," Fuzz said. "I hear a fella can get kissed off in there if he isn't careful. What business you got in there?"

"Now who's the Nosey Parker?" I asked, leaning in close and putting on my best tough-guy face. "Now listen, ducky. You never saw me. You never talked to me. Nobody like me has been around here. Remember, you're a duck, not a pigeon or a canary. If you sing, you could get mistaken for a goose. Christmas is coming, bub, and the goose is getting fat. Do I have to draw *you* a picture?"

Little beads of sweat formed on Fuzz's beak. Coco and Luci shook like they were strapped to a paint mixer. "Sure, mac," Fuzz said. "I get it. I never saw nobody. I'm no stoolie. Your secret's safe with me. I know the score. Happy trails to you. Don't worry. I got my ducks in a row."

"See that you do," I said with another hard look just so he knew I meant business. Then I turned to Coco and Luci and tipped my hat. "Ladies, I bid you adieu." They were too afraid to speak. They just bowed their heads to me and then turned away, waiting for the fox to leave the henhouse.

Five steps into the Forest of Mistletoe, the temperature dropped to something colder than an Eskimo undertaker. I thought that if Cane and Rosebud actually wanted me to waltz into the trap they were setting for me, they could have at least tried to take a little doom out of the forecast. I walked slowly so I wouldn't make as much noise, but the snow and broken branches snapping under my feet weren't making it easy. I stopped every few steps and gave a good listen, but either the woods and the wind and my imagination were playing tricks on me or I was about to be lapped up like spiked eggnog by Uncle Rumhound.

The trees were close together and blocked out most of the sky. Running up the trunk and snaking around almost every branch was an eel of mistletoe, quietly draining the life out of a tree. When the vampire plant had sucked the life out of a branch, it would toss the dry wooden corpse aside. My trail was covered in leftovers and, every once in a while, I would see a strand of mistletoe inch toward a fresh piece of plant life.

And then one of the plants saw me.

I was caught. About ten paces away and six feet up the trunk of an oak tree, a nest of mistletoe turned and looked right at me. The gnarl of branches almost had a face and the twigs gave a dry rustle like it was blinking its eyes. It was as if the plant face couldn't quite believe that someone had delivered a fresh dinner to him and he had to check his vision—or he was nearsighted. He gave a kind of hoarse growl, a low, raspy rumble, like a distant thundercloud with asthma. The noise got the attention of another vine, as big as a python with muscles like a gorilla. The vine dragged itself along a trunk to my left and whistled to a shrub just behind my right. The shrub was an ugly tangle of twigs, the bastard child of tumbleweed and a mongoose. I'm pretty sure it had teeth. I was surrounded and hoping that my green thumb had turned nice and black so I could compost this gang.

Up on the tree, the nearsighted bush crept down to the forest floor, looking to block me from running left. He slinked in between a gap of trees, kind of licking his lips and wheezing. The mistletoe vine stretched itself out to get within a few yards of me. As it pulled itself across the bark of the tree, it sounded like rats in a wall. Behind me, Tumbleweed gave a bored snort, as if I was dead already and not too tasty.

I looked around for Cane. I figured he would want to come and gloat, make some speech about how this was a fitting end to my sorry existence, and how Kringle Town would be better off once I had been turned into plant food. Actually, I was hoping Cane would arrive and humiliate me because it put off what was looking like a rotten way to go. But there was no Cane. No Rosebud. The forest was as quiet as a tomb, which was fitting.

I decided to run for it, but the mistletoe gang read my mind. Nearsighted gave a scream that didn't even belong in hell and, a second later, Python was around my legs once. Tumbleweed catapulted up with a growl and rammed into my shoulders, sending me to the ground. I kicked my legs to keep Python from wrapping my feet tight, hoping that I could somehow break free and make a run for it. Tumbleweed had other ideas though. I was reaching for a branch on the ground when the mean little weed rolled up on my neck and searched for the sweet spot. I managed to twist and throw him

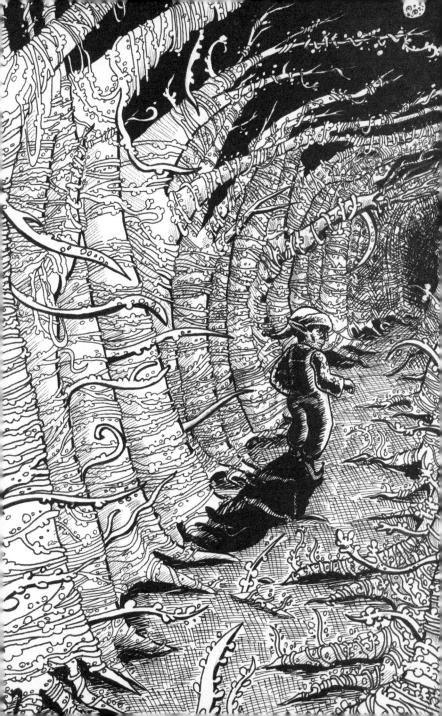

off long enough to grab a branch and whack him in the face, but the rotted wood crumbled when I hit him, only slowing him for a second. Meanwhile, my legs were getting tired and the python vine was starting to tighten the noose. Tumbleweed launched into me again and was met with a face full of elf fist. It worked better than the branch, but it also made him mad.

Over my shoulder, I noticed the nearsighted mistletoe was on the ground and crawling my way. He looked very old and brittle, making me the Senior Special. The other two plants had been sent to capture me so I could give the old bramble a proper meal. He was going to have me all to himself, the hedgehog.

I sat there thinking that the last joke I was ever going to crack was a real stinker, and that I probably deserved to die just for thinking it. But I just wished I didn't deserve it so soon.

Above me, I heard crows and vultures explode out of the trees. I figured they were too soft to watch elf carnage, but the birds were flying the coop because of the ruckus tearing through the forest and heading right for my little shindig.

As the nearsighted mistletoe geezer locked its jaws on top of my head, I smiled—

Because I spied, like every mother's child, that reindeer really do know how to fly.

CHAPTER 14

Vixen

The Christmas moose with the red beak may get all the ink, but, when push comes to shove, those in the know at the Pole go with the Originals: Dasher, Dancer, Prancer, Vixen, Comet, Cupid, Dunder (yeah, *Dunder*, not Donner) and Blitzen. Santa's A-Team is a big reason the gifts get to kids on time. Elves tip our hats to the reindeer because, without them, a lot of our toys would never make it below the tree. The reindeer are top guns; so sure, they can get a little cocky and loud. At the Blue Christmas, they hog the jukebox and stand on the bar playing air guitar. With a flashy grin and granite pecs, they'll steal your girlfriend for a few dizzy weekends in the fast lane, but she'll be just another notch on the old antler. She'll come back to you, red-eyed and ashamed, swearing that you're really the one she wants, though you'll see in her eyes that your paunch and stupid laugh make her want to heave. You'll hate a reindeer's guts for that. Many days, the reindeer are just plain jerks, flying low and knocking off your hat. They're an exclusive club and you're not allowed in. But no matter how many times they steal your girl or send you diving into the snow, when you need someone in your foxhole, there's no better sight than Santa's Caribou Cavalry coming your way.

Needless to say, it warmed my cold elf heart to see Comet motoring to my rescue, especially since it looked like he had discovered a seventh gear.

Now I know why they call Comet the "Tundra Tornado." As he barreled up to where the mistletoe monsters were getting ready to sip me until I was sapped, branches, bushes and small plants flew from Comet's wake like they had been shot out of a cannon. The air was filled with a whirl of forest shrapnel, causing my mistletoe captors to let go and dive for cover. Comet squealed into the clearing with a force so strong the mistletoe tumbleweed that seemed tough before was knocked back to Christmas Past. "If you're waiting on me, Gumdrop, you're backing up," Comet hollered. "Don't ask questions. Hop on and let's hi-ho the silver outta here."

Comet didn't have to tell me twice. I could see the

mistletoe plants around us had their backs up again and weren't going to be put off so easy. I scrambled up onto Comet's back, put an antler in each hand, and gripped them until my knuckles were white. "Giddyup," I said. Comet launched through the forest like a missile.

Comet darted between trees so closely that with every turn, I was positive I was about to become an unofficial woodpecker. At full throttle, Comet weaved through the forest, changing direction on a dime, as if he had lost his sight. But he could see plenty. Both of us could.

Vampire mistletoe plants don't take too kindly to their dinner being snatched from the table in such a rude fashion. They gave word that we were on the run and the whole forest was organizing into a life-sucking mistletoe army. Hoary plants were dropping from the branches and jumping from trunks, lashing out at Comet as he whizzed by. It seemed like every turn was blocked by a claw or wall of spindly twigs, but Comet would zip through another gap just in the nick of time. I looked behind us to see a hundred mistletoe shrubs fast on Comet's heels, fangs bared, and they were starting to spread out to surround us.

A blink later, Comet pelted past a stand of trees where a mistletoe ambush was waiting. A rugged fist of mistletoe grabbed Comet's antlers and yanked so hard Comet's head nearly came off. I held on for dear life and did the only thing I could think of: I sunk my teeth into the plant's knuckles that gripped Comet's antlers and made sure it hurt. The mistletoe pulled back with a yelp and I kicked Comet in the ribs just as a platoon of shrubs nipped at his wake.

Comet took a hard left and winged it past the reach of dark mistletoe angels raining down from the branches above. There were more mistletoe villains ahead of us and still more pushing up from the other side.

We were surrounded.

I was about to raise the white flag and jump off so Comet could escape. It was me that they wanted. But with Comet's next zigzag, I realized what he was doing.

He was tying the mistletoe into knots.

The first two batches collided in a tangle, stopping them in their tracks. The plants behind them didn't have enough time to get out of the way and flew right into a pile, creating more of a mess. Comet made one more sharp turn and sent another wave of mistletoe into the coil that would be snarled and tangled until doomsday.

"Hey, mistletoe," Comet said with a sneer. "Kiss this!" A second later, Comet launched straight up into the sky, rocketing over the trees and through the clouds to a sky so blue it brought tears to my eyes.

Or maybe I was crying for another reason. I can't remember now.

Comet was a gentleman and let me compose myself for a moment before he spoke. "You hurt?" he asked. "There was a lot of bark flying around down there. You got any splinters? Don't try and be tough; they can get infected."

"I'm fine," I said. "I could never have flown through all that stuff. I'm not strong enough. I owe you one."

Comet gave a snort. "Not me. I ain't so sure you shouldn't be hung by the chimney without care. You're an outlaw, Gumdrop, and I don't know if I like being in your company. No, this is a favor for somebody else."

"Who? Dingleberry?"

"Negative," Comet said. "Dingleberry don't talk to me since I gave him that wedgie a while back. It was just a joke, but he's still pretty steamed, so I wouldn't cross the street to help that huffy little twerp. He can suck rope for all I care."

"Who then?" I asked.

"Keep your shirt on," Comet said. "I'm to deliver you to that clearing ahead, so you'll see soon enough."

Comet swooped down a few miles later to a glade just across a river from the mistletoe forest. Apparently, killer plants can't swim because the trees just past the clearing were free from the pucker suckers. Comet barely let me climb off before he shot back into the sky without a word. I was alone with nothing but the sound of wind and water.

I don't know why I didn't fly away right then. Nothing was stopping me and it wasn't like staying was a good idea. Still, something told me to hang around for a while. I had the feeling I was being watched. My guess was that whoever was watching me was in the woods, but I had my fill of forest for the moment. I decided to walk to the river and empty my head.

The water was clear and cold; the current moved fast. It looked deep too. The view up and downstream gave me no idea how far I was from anywhere, and I wondered if my rescue wasn't a rescue at all. I wondered if Cane thought I'd be afraid to show my mug in Kringle Town and that I would choose just to starve to death by this river. Cane might have also hoped that I would become some kind of vampire from a mistletoe's kiss, making me a threat to come after Cane. There ain't no silver bullets in Kringle Town. But why would he send Comet to rescue me? To get me to trust him? There were too many thoughts taking laps in my head.

I mean, I could fly if I needed to, but there was nowhere to go. Nor was I too keen on the idea of being up in the reindeer's airspace. If Comet was giving me the cold shoulder, I shivered at the thought of a dogfight with Prancer. As I pondered all of this and the mess I had gotten myself into, I did what anyone would do while pondering: I skipped rocks.

The riverbed was full of them. They were the perfect

size and as smooth as velvet. Using a sidearm toss, I whipped the first stone across the water—one, two, three, four, *plunk!* I couldn't help but smile. I sent another rock flying—seven hops before it slid into the water as quiet as a seal. Now I was going to have to break my record. I curled my finger around a stone and flung it, snapping my wrist like it had a spring in it. The rock hummed across the river, kissing the top of the water— one, two, three, four, five. Another rock whistled past mine, spraying water like some kind of Neptune pixie before it slipped into the water after eight skips. I turned around to see who or what launched the stone, but there was no one there.

I reached back to throw another rock, but before I could even get into my windup, another stone came from behind me and danced across the water like it had wings. It plopped across the water nine or ten times, cutting somersaults. Show-off.

Again, I turned around. "Pretty cute," I said to no one. "If you think you can spook me, you're going to have to try harder." My answer was a rock that socked my bottom lip. It came from nowhere and skipped off my chin just as easily as it did the water. It stung and it scared me, and I had a hard time not showing it. My hands went to catch the blood and I screamed, "LEAVE ME ALONE! LEAVE ME ALONE!"

After my echo finished ricocheting off the trees for a

few minutes, I had to sit and listen to myself sniffle in the quiet. I couldn't stop. I was beat and they, whoever they were, knew it.

"Boy, I thought someone said the bigger they are, the harder they fall, but I guess a shrimp boat can hit the iceberg too."

I looked up and saw Rosebud Jubilee. She was working a peppermint stick with that pretty little mouth, and the cocksure rake of her hat seemed like it was mocking me. She had a handful of rocks. "Put some snow on that bottom lip and it won't be so bad. Sorry about that, toots. My aim's a little off."

I did as I was told. The snow was cold, but it numbed the pain. "What were you aiming for?"

"Your upper lip," she said with a smirk.

"Cute."

"It's about time you noticed, Coal," Rosebud said.

"Oh, I noticed before," I said. I felt like I had one good tussle left in me. "I just figured there was no point since you were writing 'Mrs. Candy Cane' in the margins of your notebook."

"I never figured you for reading the gossip column, Coal. You read 'Advice to the Lovelorn' too?"

"Sure, I want to see if they answer my letter."

"Did you sign it 'Short on Romance'?"

"Nope," I said. "I signed it 'Size Matters.' They haven't printed it."

"Must have been your purple prose. I guess that leaves you kind of blue," Rosebud said.

"What kind of colorful language does Cane woo you with?" I asked. "Does he whisper sweet nothings in your ear or hypnotize you by dangling some sparkling ambition in front of you?"

"Green is not a good color for you, Gumdrop," Rosebud said. "It clashes with your lederhosen."

"You can't blame me for being jealous," I said, taking a step toward her. "I mean, how's an elf like me supposed to compete with Santa's bright boy? Cane is a big man in Kringle Town and I'm nothing. You might say we're polar opposites." I was close to her now and I could tell she was getting a touch nervous. I liked that, so I leaned in more. "Cane is a giant among elves."

"Maybe size doesn't matter," Rosebud said.

"Maybe you want to prove it," I said and bent forward for a kiss.

That's when Rosebud slapped me so hard across the face I felt a molar bruise. "You're gonna have to work a little harder than that before you drop down my chimney, Gumdrop Coal," Rosebud said. Her back was up, but she was still smiling. "My being here is what proves I'm on your side, you nincompoop."

"So you and Cane can rub me out together?" I asked, rubbing my jaw.

"Cane and the rest of Kringle Town are still looking

for you in Whoville, thanks to me," Rosebud said. "I sent you that note because I knew the route to the mistletoe forest wasn't being watched. No one thinks you're stupid enough to go to the woods."

I figured Rosebud slapped me harder than I thought because I was confused. "Are you trying to tell me that the mistletoe forest wasn't a trap set by you and Cane?"

"That's right, sugarplum," Rosebud said. "Momma has been undercover all this time to save your little hide, because you're in over your head and you don't even know it. You think you're the only one who can turn invisible? You don't have to be a Zwarte Pieten for that, toots. I know you didn't deck the Hall schmuck, but I do think Cane knows who swiped Ralphie's Red Ryder and shot him. I also think Cane will let you take the fall for it. He's had your number for a long time and wants you out of the way. I'm just now sure about the why of it all."

"How do you know all this?"

"Like every other alpha elf at the North Pole, Cane will talk a country mile to the fairer sex if he thinks it will lead to some stocking stuffing," Rosebud said with a matter-of-fact shrug. "There's a holy mackerel of a story here, and I'm the girl who's gonna reel it in, buster. I don't know what Cane's scheme is exactly, but I know part of it was getting rid of the Coal Patrol and then punching you a one-way ticket to Banditoville. Cane thinks that my hanging on his every word is a bad case of puppy love and I let him think it. But what I was really doing was listening and waiting for the puzzle pieces to spit out of that pretty mouth of his."

"All for a story?" I asked. Despite the ache in my jaw, I leaned back toward Rosebud and took a swim in her eyes.

She smiled and leaned forward herself. "It's a big story, Coal. I think the Fat Man's in real danger and somehow you and Cane are in the middle of it. If I can break the story and help save Santa, I'll be swimming in gravy."

Every time someone mentioned Santa getting the bump, I got a bad case of heartburn. Was this really what all this was about? "So you're playing Cane," I said. "How do I know I'm not just another road to your story?"

In her own ladylike way, Rosebud Jubilee spit out the peppermint stick, slung an arm around my neck and kissed me. She kissed me like we were both meant for this one moment, and my hunch was she was right. After a few minutes of pure heaven, she pulled back and gave me a smile. "Because I love ya, you big lummox. Well, little lummox."

"Seems kinda quick. On the record?"

"And on the level," Rosebud said in a way that made

me want to believe her. "Don't let your head swell, but I've been watching you for a while because Cane has been pulling strings for months. At first, I just thought you were kind of a lovable jerk, but when I saw that you were being set up, I kinda got a soft spot for you. I still think you're a jerk and stupid, but I'd wager there's more to the story of Gumdrop Coal."

"And you want to write the sappy ever after," I said.

"Something like that, yeah."

"So instead of going to Santa or Bert the Cop and telling them that I am innocent in all this, you send me to the mistletoe forest, where I almost become a botany buffet? You then rescue me by sending me on a joyride with a crazed reindeer rocket. Then you throw a rock at my lip and smack me hard enough to take plaque off my teeth. That's how you let a guy know you're interested?"

"You'd rather have a card with kittens on it?" Rosebud said.

"It doesn't make sense."

"Apparently, your tinsel doesn't go all the way to the top," Rosebud said. "First, I wasn't completely sure you were innocent until I knew that Hall's eye had been shot out. I was there, Gumdrop, invisible and standing right beside you. I don't think you're clever enough to come up with something so subtle. If you were going to ice someone, you'd be all tough about it and use your fist or a piece of lumber. Second, I could tell by the look on your face that you were innocent and that you knew you were being set up. I've been studying that mug of yours for quite a while and can read you like a *By George* comic book. I followed you to Ralphie, honey. I stayed invisible because if Cane had any idea we were together, he'd clam up and torpedo my story. When you started to head to Whoville, I was able to put some pieces together. Cane took a call from Lou Who a couple of weeks ago when we were having dinner. I went to talk to Lou Who but found him knocked out."

"The sugar coma," I said.

"Yeah, all the clues point to Cane," she said. "But something is not right."

"What do you mean?" I asked. "Your boyfriend sugar talks to Lou Who to keep him quiet."

"Only I don't think he did it," Rosebud said. "Cane talks good, but he doesn't close any deal. I've been alone with him, you know? He just can't seem to bring himself to kiss me. He'll spew hearts and flowers 'til pigs fly, but he never brings home the bacon, if you know what I mean? No killer instinct. Something told me to get you out of the way to give me a little more time. I led you to the mistletoe forest for safety and slipped Comet some dough to keep an eye on you."

"Ukulele Who said a dame took care of Lou," I said in a way that let Rosebud know I still wasn't convinced.

"And a duck told me he saw an elf and a good-looking honey go into the mistletoe forest the other day."

"I don't know who Ukulele is talking about, but the duck's on the up and up, and he has good taste," Rosebud said. "That was me and Dingleberry."

"You got Dingleberry mixed up in all of this?" I asked.

"Oh, sweetie," Rosebud said. "This is where it gets good."

CHAPTER 15

Grown a Little Colder

THE MARSHMALLOW WORLD GAZETTE

Santa Agrees to Reexamine Treaty with Misfit Toys

Staff Writer

Misfit Isle officials have asked the Office of Santa Toy Standards to attend a summit regarding the banishment of Misfit Toys. With this year's increased demand for toys, Misfit Isle believes there could be an opportunity to place slightly maligned toys with children. Santa has agreed to listen. Centuries ago, Santa established Misfit Isle as a state for damaged or poorly received playthings. "I do not enjoy the idea of separating the

Misfit Toys," Santa said. "But I believe good children deserve the best toys possible. I feel that if a Misfit Toy was given to a child, the child would be disappointed and the toy abused." Misfit Toys once lived freely throughout Kringle Town until violence on elves and other toys compromised the order and safety of the community. Though there have been brief moments of civil unrest every few years, relations between Kringle Town and Misfit Isle have been peaceful. This is the first time Misfit Isle has proposed a treaty change. "I believe dis is a great opportunity for zee Misfit," said Zsa Zsa Schnitzel, one of the organizers of the summit. "I tink Santa vill see that zee Misfits can make vittle children very happy." Santa plans to visit Misfit Isle a few days before Christmas Eve. "I'll listen to what they have to say, but I'm making no promises," he said. "A child should know his or her toy is perfect."

I could tell Kringle Town was in a dark mood when we found Dingleberry Fizz up to his elbow in the cookie jar. I hope you won't lose any sleep when I tell you that Santa doesn't eat all of those cookies you leave for him. He just can't. First, there's the whole "Naughty Cholesterol" issue. Second, most of your cookies are inedible, merciless, granite globs of sugar and lard, a kind of cookie jerky whipped up at the last minute before bed. Elves use those cookies for roof shingles and patios. Of the thousands and thousands of good cookies, Santa will take a nibble just to be polite, but then brings the rest of the batch back to the North Pole and puts them in the elves' huge cookie pantry. Most of you cubicle convicts serve your time with the help of a java or a soda pop. Elves are fueled by sugar. Cookies, candy, cakes, pies—an elf's sweet tooth is primal and not picky. Need six million Poopy Droopy Diaper Dolls with Wipe-Away Rash by sundown? Toss a handful of elves a couple of sleeves of chocolate chip cookies and get out of the way. During the Christmas of '88, when it seemed like every tyke in the hemisphere was clamoring for the Z-Box's *Grandma Hostage Ninja Rescue*, Santa stepped up production with a few dozen rhubarb pies and a turbocharged hot chocolate. Because Santa brings back thousands of sweets every Christmas morning, elves are able to snag a bite of some sugar goodness whenever we want. Of course, Dingleberry is also a stress eater. The pile of crumbs told me Dingleberry was in a dither. He burst into tears when he saw me.

I imagine that I was quite a sight. Not taking a chance with her big story, Rosebud snuck me back into Kringle Town through a hopscotch of other holiday worlds. You'd think Halloween Town would be the worst, but, believe me, you don't want to spend any more time than you have to on the *Pinta* in Columbus Day City. Scurvy will be the least of your problems. Dingleberry rushed over and soaked my shoulder with a fresh spring of tears and mucus. "What have they done to you?! I'm so sorry I said those things, Gum-drop," he said. "You're my best friend and I doubted you. You really are good, better than George, even. Well, almost. You can hate me the rest of your life if you want, but I'll still be your best friend." Dingleberry cried some more while I patted his shoulder.

"Doesn't anybody want to talk about football?" Rosebud asked. "Or trucks?"

After a few minutes, I got Dingleberry to cork the waterworks so he could tell me what I had missed.

"Tell him what you told me," Rosebud said like she didn't have all day.

Suddenly, Dingleberry looked scared to death and he swallowed hard to keep from coming unglued all over again. He looked at me with big eyes and a lip that wouldn't sit still and whispered, "Gumdrop. Mr. Cane is stealing *toys*!"

It sounded daffy. "Toys? Why would any elf steal toys?" I said. "They play with them all day long! Dingle-berry, you're one of the few that isn't sick to death of toys."

"Cane's not playing with toys, tough guy," Rosebud said. "Finish it, Ding."

Dingleberry slowly pulled a folded piece of paper from inside his shirt. He held it gently like it might explode. "It's the Misfit Mafia." Dingleberry said the name quietly, as if he would actually summon them if he said it any louder. "I came back the night of our fight, but you were gone. I found this on your doormat. The note was open, but it was wrong of me to peek. I'm sorry."

"Stop saying you're sorry, Dingleberry." I read the note:

Dear Gumdrop,

The game's afoot! I have deduced that there really is a Misfit Mafia! Great Caesar's Ghost! I may need your help, so stay close!

Sherlock Stetson

P.S. Zsa Zsa says hello to her vittle Gumdrop and that if you've got the chimney sweeper, she's got the flue. Don't worry; I'll get her some soup.

"Did you read this?" I asked Rosebud.

"You bet your buttons I did, my vittle Gumdrop. Please tell me you didn't jingle all the way with Frau Floozy," Rosebud said. "It would break my heart and I'd have to burn my lips off."

"No presents were unwrapped," I said. "I wasn't even curious enough to peek. But what does Sherlock's note have to do with Cane stealing toys?"

"Cane is part of the Misfit Mafia," Dingleberry said. "He's stealing toys for them. I know he is!"

"But why?" Rosebud said. "That's what I don't understand. There's never been any proof that the Misfit Mafia existed, much less this organized. Why would Cane get Gumdrop out of the way and frame him for a murder just to steal toys? I can only think of one reason, but I hope I'm wrong. What do you think, Coal?"

I let Rosebud's question chase an answer around in my noggin, but I didn't like what I kept catching. The only thing I could figure was a lot worse than I could ever imagine. A lot worse. And it made me mad and sick to my stomach.

"Cane wants to be Santa Claus," I said like it was a curse. Dingleberry started crying again and Rosebud shook her head no.

"That's what I thought too, but Cane doesn't have it in him, I tell ya," she said. "Make your case."

"He who has the most toys wins," I said. "Cane wants to be liked, to be beloved. Who's more loved than Santa? Cane wants the power to make children happy and for them to love him. The Misfit Mafia is a fake. Like Santa, Cane's not going to unload a lot of junk on kids. They wouldn't adore him and that's what Cane wants. But the difference between Cane and Claus, or Santa and anybody really, is that Santa really and truly cares about the kids, not the adulation. In fact, caring so much about the kids' happiness is what is killing Santa, wearing him out. The only thing standing in Santa's way of doing more for years has been . . ."

"Gumdrop Coal," Dingleberry said.

"Bingo," I said. "As long as there was a Naughty List, Santa would not have to worry about giving something to every single kid in the world. But get me and my old-fashioned notions out of the way, and the Fat Man's got a ton of toys to make."

"And he wears himself out doing it," Dingleberry said with a sniffle. "You should see him too. He looks like he could fade away any second!"

"There wouldn't be a drop of blood on Cane's lily-white hands." Rosebud said the last part, and, for the first time since I'd known her, she looked scared. "And then Cane just slithers on in, tells Santa he'll take care of everything while the old man naps or—" Rosebud stopped breathing.

"Or the Fat Man goes beard up," I said, finishing her awful thought. All of us were quiet for a bit after that. We were trying not to imagine a world without Santa Claus. Santa was the only goodness some kids knew. Once a year, hope came in the form of a toy truck or teddy bear. Santa made it possible for kids to understand the true meaning of Christmas. To a kid, the gift the Child gave the world is a little too much to understand. Everlasting life doesn't mean much when you're six. But as kids get older, and they hear Christmas's old, old story, they start connecting that toy that made them feel special to the Child in the manger—the gift that lets us know that we are all special. Like clutching that teddy bear, the Child gives us peace, a presence, a feeling to cling to in the dark. His gift is wonderful, made just for you and your happiness. Going from believing in Santa to believing in the Child is an easy step because Santa shows us that we can all reflect the light of the Child if we try. Even if we're naughty, Santa finds a way to forgive and give. How could I forget that? Santa shows the joy that comes with giving. Take the bridge from Santa to the Child away and the road to believing in anything good is a dead end.

Now I was scared.

"We need to tell Santa," Dingleberry said.

"I don't think he'd believe me," I said. "Cane's done a pretty good job of framing me. No, Candy Cane's going to have to confess."

"How are you going to get him to spill?" Rosebud asked.

"We're going to frolic and play, the Eskimo way," I said.

"What does that mean?" Dingleberry asked.

"I think the phrase 'cold-blooded' might have something to do with it," Rosebud said.

"You need to be careful, Gumdrop," Dingleberry

said. "Mr. Cane is not taking any chances. Since no one has found you yet, he's locked himself up with the toys and put a guard outside."

"After the Forest of Mistletoe, I think I can take care of a guard," I replied with as much strut as I could manage.

"Not this one," Dingleberry said. He reached into his pocket, pulled something out and tossed it to me. When I caught a pecan, I knew who Cane's guard was and I winced at the pain heading my way.

"Oh, Tannenbomb."

CHAPTER 16

Oh, Tannenbomb

Dingleberry and Rosebud were fine with me going after Candy Cane all by my lonesome, but they would not hear of me taking on Tannenbomb solo, and I was in no position to argue. Not only was my engine sputtering on fumes, Tannenbomb was a serious piece of bad news.

Guarding Candy Cane was a monster nutcracker, a twenty-two-foot Amazon shell splitter who killed for peanuts. Legend has it that the oak Tannenbomb was carved from was struck by a mean bolt of lightning, spiking the wood with a hard-boiled venom that the devil himself envied, turning the nutcracker into one sadistic assassin for hire. Fire, silver-bladed axes, termites— nothing could defeat Tannenbomb, so Santa and Kringle

Town's finest always tried to keep him occupied with long hunts in the wilderness for the Rat King. If Tannenbomb were half as smart as he is strong, he'd know he was on a snipe hunt, but his brain is mostly driftwood, so the ruse has worked for years. I don't know how Cane found Tannenbomb and trained him to take orders, but he did it. There Tannenbomb stood, guarding the inner sanctum of Cane's Xanadu lair and there was no getting around him. The clap of his wooden jaw sounded like your casket closing.

I was feeling about as tough as a Sugarplum Fairy.

Still, I had to do something. Cane was hiding behind the door ahead of me, thousands of toys with him, hoarding them so he could be the new Santa once the Fat Man shriveled up from exhaustion. I was the only one who could stop Candy Cane's plan, but when I looked up at the Cashew King Kong I literally hoped I wasn't, well, nuts.

"Here goes nothing," I told Dingleberry and Rosebud. "I'm making this up as I go along, so just listen and watch. And pray."

I stepped into the entrance hall of Cane's private quarters. The room was huge, the walls as tall as a canyon. In the middle was a Christmas tree, one of the biggest ones I'd ever seen. It was so big Tannenbomb looked like a toy beside it. The tree was decorated with large golden balls, millions of them, and about thirty miles of silver tinsel. The gaudiness made my stomach churn. It looked like the tree of a robber baron. I came around the tree and faced the nutcracker, but Tannenbomb stared straight ahead, a good soldier. He didn't even see me, so I thought I could possibly tiptoe around him. I took a few quiet steps to my right, keeping my eyes on the nutcracker.

I should have kept at least one eye on where I was going because less than ten steps away from the door, I walked all over a pile of discarded pecan shells. The noise sounded like a T. rex cracking its back.

Tannenbomb flared his nostril with a perturbed snort, and the growl that boiled out of his chest sounded like a freight train with a toothache. A hard, merciless eye found me among the nutshells, but it warmed when Tannenbomb realized he had something to kill. He lifted a boot to smash me.

Tannenbomb was quicker than I thought. As his foot came down, I dove forward as fast as I could, but felt the whoosh of the near miss run up my back like an ill wind. Splinters of pecan shells rained through the air like arrows, so, instead of standing up and running, I had to crawl like a bug scampering for a dark place to hide. Cane's door was only a few feet away, but it might as well have been at the South Pole. In the next blink, Tannenbomb's broadsword swept me across the room like a ball of dust.

The world was spinning and listing starboard, but I knew better than to sit still. I could feel Tannenbomb stomping toward me, so I got to my feet and let my legs do the best they could. Above me was Tannenbomb's open hand, big and not looking as cozy as I had hoped. I gave my head a shake to clear my eyes and guessed I would have a chance if I zigzagged at Tannenbomb's feet. I guessed right.

As a rule, giant monster nutcrackers made of solid wood are not as nimble as the dancers that play them in the ballet. It takes a lot of effort to swing that lumber around, and Tannenbomb was about a second late. And a second was all I needed.

I darted between Tannenbomb's legs, put my hand on the door handle and yanked. The door came to me, but then slammed back into place. Tannenbomb had returned the door with a thump of his paw and bounced me back into the middle of the room. I was a sitting duck.

Tannenbomb's arm was about to fly down and slap me redheaded, when a pecan bounced off his noggin. I turned to see Dingleberry with an empty, guilty slingshot. Rosebud was beside him, ready to heave another handful of nuts at the giant. "Step away from the elf, stick boy," Rosebud said with a snarl. "Or Momma will huff and puff and blow your house down."

I'm pretty sure Dingleberry wet himself just then.

I wasn't so sure how long I was going to stay dry either.

At first Tannenbomb looked hurt at Rosebud's remark, as if she'd told him their romance was over and that she had fallen for a marionette. *"It was beauty that killed the beast."* Getting past Tannenbomb was going to be easier than I thought.

But just as I let out the tiniest of breaths, the big nut ape reached down and swooped up Rosebud in his mitt and held her above his head at what looked like cloud level. I was back at the drawing board and running out of chalk.

Rosebud screamed like a cold shower. Since I had known her, Rosebud had always been flatline calm, but I guessed that when a twenty-foot nutcracker is looking at you like you're a goober to be gobbled, you're allowed to have a hissy fit or two. She kicked and squirmed, pounding her tiny fist on Tannenbomb's big wooden fingers. "AAAAAAAAGHHHHHHHHHHHH!" she screamed loud enough to be heard on Pluto, but Tannenbomb could only hear his heart skipping a beat.

"GUMDROP," Rosebud yelled with bloody tonsils. "DO SOMETHING!"

Dingleberry was frozen. Apparently, years of studying every heroic feat of *By George* had not prepared Ding for actual combat. In desperation, Dingleberry flung his empty slingshot at Tannenbomb, but his nerves had gotten to him and Ding couldn't hit soot if he fell down a chimney. I needed to think of something fast because it was starting to look like the nutcracker wanted to be alone with Rosebud and that meant sending Dingleberry and me to Shell Town. But how do you hurt a sequoia?

You get the sequoia to chop itself down.

"Follow me," I said to Dingleberry. "Watch me carefully and do what I do." I didn't wait for him to ask for more instructions and I jumped into the air like a rocket with good old wonderfully loyal Dingleberry right behind me.

We made a wide circle around Tannenbomb's gigantic head, buzzing by close enough to get his attention. His empty hand went to swat us down, but we inched up in altitude just out of reach. This made Tannenbomb mad, and he lurched at us, jumping as high as he could, which wasn't much.

With Dingleberry right behind, I made a wider circle and came around the giant tree, hooking one of the golden ornaments with my hand. I zoomed back to the sky above Tannenbomb, dropping the ornament so it would hit Tannenbomb square on the head.

Bull's-eye.

Dingleberry did the same, landing a direct hit.

Our elf air force came around again a few more times, launching ornament bombs at the big ape with all the fight we had in us. Golden glass rained like a rainbow had exploded. The only thing louder than the ornaments crashing was Rosebud's shrieks. She was either scared out of her mind by now, or was trying for some kind of record.

Tannenbomb was getting steamed, using his one free hand to slice the air like a madman shooing away flies. Dingleberry and I kept just out of his grasp, but Tannenbomb wasn't giving up. He put Rosebud on his shoulder, grabbed the huge Christmas tree and started to climb. Every few feet, he'd grip the tree with one hand and take a swing at me and Dingleberry, but we were too quick for him.

"Keep throwing those ornaments, Ding," I hollered. "And keep making him climb. Just watch that big hand of his."

"Roger," Dingleberry said. "Bogey is padlocked and I'm kicking up to warp one for a knife fight in a phone booth with fangs out, over."

"Dingleberry, why are you talking like that?"

"In issue 988 of *By George Adventures—Mangy Dogfight,* George joined Captain Billy 'Souptooth' Cigar's air squadron and he talked like that," Dingleberry said. "I've always wanted to say that."

Tannenbomb continued to climb and Rosebud seemed to scream louder for every foot he made it up the tree, but, from my point of view, things were going according to Hoyle. The higher Tannenbomb got, the

more the big balsam shook. Decorations were starting to rattle off and all the noise and the mess was putting bats in the big nutcracker's belfry. When he slapped the angel off the top and grabbed the roof of the tree, I knew we had him. Me and Dingle went around in a wide circle, flinging ornaments and blowing raspberries. Tannenbomb roared like a grizzly and thrashed the air like an unhinged windmill. Rosebud held on for dear life, her lungs raw. The breaking point wouldn't be long in coming.

About the time I finished that thought, Tannenbomb let go of the tree and lunged at Dingleberry, missing him completely. Tannenbomb hung in the air for a brief second, in a lather that he missed the little elf-fly again, but then he realized that his world wasn't as solid as it used to be. He quickly turned to Rosebud, looking at her for what he knew would be the last time. It would have been sweet had it not been so ridiculous. Then, Tannenbomb simply gave up and let gravity take over. He shot to the earth like a lame comet, ornaments and tinsel and branches exploding in his wake. Rosebud had enough wits about her to let go and, when she did, I swooped in like one of those guys in a cape and caught her midair. I was feeling pretty good about my heroics, but Rosebud gave me a cold slap of krypton. "Remind me to get you a watch, Coal. What took you so long?"

"Timber!" Dingleberry yelled, happy as a clam.

When Tannenbomb hit the ground it sounded like a couple of bowling alleys having a fender bender. Wooden arms and legs snapped with a boom, the logs crashing into each other so hard you could feel it in your teeth. Tannenbomb's mouth lever cracked and bounced across the floor, causing his mighty jaw to fall slack and harmless. He was dead.

Rosebud, Dingleberry and I landed beside the heap and stared at Tannenbomb, all stumps and splinters. "Welcome to the Termite Buffet," Rosebud said.

"Getting rid of Tannenbomb ought to help your case with Santa, Gumdrop," Dingleberry said to me. "He's been causing Kringle Town trouble for years!"

"The only thing that's going to get me out of Dutch with Nick is proving that I didn't kill Hall," I said. "So let's go see if Candy Cane can help me."

"You know what's funny?" Rosebud asked. "All that racket right outside his door and not a peep from Cane."

"What do you think it means?"

Rosebud started moving as she answered. "I think it means we better open this door."

CHAPTER 17

A Long Winter's Nap

Even for an elf who's helped load the sleigh on Christmas Eve, the amount of toys crammed into Charles "Candy" Cane's mansion made my mouth drop open. Xanadu was a tall canyon of a joint, big enough to have a bus line. And almost every inch of it was taken up with toys. Games, dolls, balls, trucks and bikes were stacked floor to ceiling, three stories high. Stuffed animals of every breed clung to small cliffs on the toy mountain like avalanche survivors. A trail about three hairs wide trickled between the great walls of toys. It was dark and didn't look safe, but from the other end we heard the wheeze of someone measuring his last breaths.

"You weren't kidding, were you, Dingleberry," I said. "Cane was hoarding toys. Now it all makes sense. Cane got me out of the way because as long as I was about naughty children, not as many toys got made. So when every kid in the world gets what they want, production has to ramp up. Cane starts to skim while Santa works himself to death. Suddenly, Santa's too tired to take care of Christmas and Cane's got a storehouse of toys. Like a white knight, he rides in, saves Christmas Day and, like Rudolph, goes down in history."

"And to think I helped him do it!" Dingleberry cried. "Me and the other elves worked triple shifts to make more and more toys and didn't notice Cane was taking them until it was too late. Santa is just as sick as he can be!"

At that, Rosebud and I looked at each other having the same awful thought. The wheezing we heard coming deep from the maze of toys was Santa's. A second later, the three of us dove down the trail, trying to hear the hiss of a dying breath over the pounding thump of our heartbeats.

Santa couldn't die. It wasn't possible. It wasn't right. He wasn't just a jolly old elf and toymaker. He was God's own angel, sent here to show the spirit of Christmas to the poor souls too stubborn or stupid or scared to step into a church. Believing Santa could deliver gifts to the whole world in a single night made it possible to believe that on one quiet night, God gave the whole world the greatest gift. That notion would get in people's craw and it would never go away. It might get quiet, the noise of the world might drown it out, but hearing Santa's "Ho ho ho!" and seeing his rosy cheeks would make them remember. And when someone gave another person a gift, when they played Santa, and saw their friend's eyes light up with surprise, their hearts might just get a little air under them. Then maybe, just maybe, they would learn and know and believe. Santa couldn't stop and he couldn't be replaced by Cane. Cane would poison it. Piling presents up on a kid made the presents and the kid worthless. The giv-ing would no longer be a blessing. It had to remain special. It had to be something you believed in more than you could hold. A wish that would make you know you were special. Santa knew how to make that kind of gift because he put his good, beautiful and pure heart into it. I ran faster because Santa wasn't going to die on my watch.

I finally rounded a corner and the walls opened up into a small, cluttered room. I saw a gray hooded figure standing over a man on his deathbed. It was the end of my world.

"Whose bottom do you have to butter to get a cup of tea around here, old chap?" the specter chirped. The question caught me up short and I stopped where I stood. Dingleberry and Rosebud plowed into me, but I didn't feel a thing. I just stared at the faceless figure. Under the hood was a black hole, an inky, endless pit with nothing in it but a couple pins of orange light for eyes. "You would think in a palace of this sort, a bloke could find something for whistle wetting, but chaps in the Foreign Legion are more dewy than me, I'd wager," said the voice coming from the faceless black hole.

"Are you talking to me?" I asked, trying to make some sense of everything.

"Well, I'm not talking to *him*," the phantom said, pointing a long, spindly finger at the man in the bed gasping for breath. I followed the finger and saw that the dying man was not Santa. It was Cane! "What's wrong with him?"

"Oh he's dying, I'm afraid," the phantom said with a shrug of the shoulders. "Buying the farm, expiring, his candle has a reservation in Snuff Town, so if you've come to say farewell, you've ankled in here just in the nick, believe me."

"Are you the Angel of Death?" Dingleberry asked, his eyes wide with wonder.

"Oh no, ducky," said the figure. "I'm the Ghost of Christmas Yet to Come. Angel of Death needed a few days off. I can't say that I blame him. Escorting chaps to the Finis Express can get dreary day in and day out. Even if a bloke is tossing the old mortal coil for an eternal romp behind the Pearlies, one must endure quite a spot of melancholy digging of the heels, gnashing of teeth, that sort of thing. It can be quite tiresome, so Death took a holiday and I am his able substitute. I say, that was rather good for speech extemporary—*Death took a holiday*. Must share that with the missus, ha!"

The Ghost of Christmas Yet to Come's explanation of events aggravated Cane's dying. His breath got raspier and hurried, and he fidgeted and thrashed in his bed. His eyes were wide with fear and he mumbled something, but I couldn't catch what.

"He's been carrying on like this since I arrived," Ghost said. He turned to Cane and cooed, "Settle still, there, Master Cane. Think of tranquil waters and kittens or something. Try and spy the light, ducky. Spy the light." Ghost then turned to us, lowered his voice and said, "Of course, in his case, I believe, for him, *the light* means the roaster is preheated and ready to begin never-ending poach, poor sot."

"Maybe I can lower the temperature for him some," I said and moved to Cane. Gone was the elf who was going to take over the world. Everything about Cane was gray: his hair, his skin and his eyes. He was trembling and searching for a sight or sound of comfort. "Cane," I said in the friendliest voice I could muster, "it's Gumdrop Coal. Do you remember me?"

Cane's eyes told me that he knew who I was, but my

presence wasn't helping. He probably thought I was there to finish him off. "I'm going to offer you a chance for a little redemption, Candy," I told him. "Now that I have witnesses, just tell me if you cooked up this plan, killing Raymond Hall and framing me, to take over Kringle Town and become Santa. Just give the nod and you'll feel better for it."

Cane nodded right away. But he nodded "no."

"Pants on fire!" Ghost said. "Well, they're about to be, quite literally."

At first, I wanted to punch Cane, but my gut told me that someone with the bucket right in front of their boot would tell the truth. Even Cane wasn't stupid enough to think he could lie his way out of this one. "Do you know who did do it?" I asked.

This time, Cane's head went vertical. "Yes," he said in a hoarse whisper. "Yes."

"Well, out with it already, poodle," Ghost said, giving Cane a poke with his bony finger. "Don't think a drawn-out deathbed confession is going to stretch your life taffy. I have a schedule to keep."

I shot Ghost a look to stifle it, and turned back to Cane. "Did someone put you up to the frame-up? Who *was* it?"

Cane's eyes half-closed and he took a long swallow. He lifted his hand like it was made of stone and pointed over my shoulder. "Rosebud," he said.

My heart stopped. It had to because it broke right then and there.

Cane's arm dropped back to his side and he looked at me, pleading for help. He was probably the saddest thing I had ever seen, but at that moment, I would have swapped places.

"He's lying," Rosebud said behind me. "Gumdrop, you know it's not true."

"Do I?"

"Why would I do such a thing?" she asked.

I turned around. Rosebud's face was red, but her jaw was set in granite. She looked like she expected me to believe her or that she would smack me around until I did. "Why? Because it would make a good story, that's why. You said it yourself; you want a big story. Candy shares his ambition and you smell front-page ink. But when you discover Cane doesn't have the brainpower to pull off such a caper and make for good reading, you whisper a little sweet nothing that he needs to get me out of the way and help him along. Ukulele Who said a dame got to Lou Who. So, you get Ralphie's rifle, give Raymond Hall the powder and type up that little poem on your typewriter, framing me for the murder or framing Cane for the framing. You're fixed both ways. Then you give Lou Who just enough sugar to put him in a diabetic coma. To cover your bases, you lead me to the mistletoe forest, rescue me, get my trust. Plus all the while, your story gets bigger and bigger. My guess is that Tannenbomb was to pecan me out there. I bet you thought you'd be at a typewriter right now. Or you've already got it written and are waiting to put in the final adjectives. Yeah, it's all making sense now. You'd say the nutcracker went nuts when I killed his master, Cane. It actually ties up pretty neat."

"Rosebud," Cane croaked again.

"Shut up, Candy!" Rosebud said. "He's talking out of his head, Gumdrop, and so are you. Use that brain of yours. If I would have just left you for dead in the mistletoe forest, I could have written the story any old way I wanted. I wouldn't need to go to all this trouble with Cane."

"Except that Cane knew what you were up to," I said. "And Dingleberry knew that Cane was stealing toys. Cane figured he might get caught and he was up to his neck. You knew he wouldn't survive a third degree, so you wrote a different ending. A pretty splashy one, to boot. My hunch is that even though he's a pompous twit, you knew Cane didn't have the backbone to lie for you, so you went to work."

"Rosebud!" Cane wheezed.

"This is all very 'Colonel Horseradish in the library with the Balzac,' but we're wasting time," Ghost said, clapping his hands like a nanny. "I've got to attend to the expiration of a grandma at the expense of a reindeer and some fatally poked cowpoke, so we really need Citizen Cane to start pushing the proverbial daisies with a little more gusto."

"Gumdrop Coal, someone has rung your silver bell," Rosebud said, madder than I had ever seen her. "Your thinking's not so merry and bright. What would happen after that? I'd have to kill Dingleberry and he's clearly been above ground."

"Except that you led us both into a fight with a giant nutcracker," I shot back. "Pretty sweet how Tannenbomb scooped you up to get you out of the way so you wouldn't get hurt. You just didn't count on us getting past him or Cane still being alive to stool on you."

"Rosebud," Cane said again. He was weak but desperate to get the word out. Rosebud shot forward and bent down in Cane's face. "Why do you keep saying 'Rosebud'? You know I had nothing to do with Hall's murder or your plans. You're doing this to get back at me for turning you down. If you can't have me, then nobody else can, is that it? I'm sorry Cane, but you're not my cup of cocoa. Sorry if I let you believe otherwise, and sorry you fell so hard. I can't blame you. I let you believe that I was a present aching to be unwrapped, but you should have shook the box a couple of times. You'd have heard behind all the sweet talk there was nothing beneath my ribbon but a hard-boiled newspaper-woman who knows how you can't use your brain when you have only one thing on your mind. It's a heck of a thing to learn before you're about to slip on the pine kimono, but if you want to die in peace, you'll sit up right now and tell Gumdrop the truth. Do it now, or I'll start playing a little chin music on that glass jaw of yours, and believe me, I feel a symphony coming on!"

The dame had quite a mouth on her. I loved her. Too bad she was trying to kill me. For his part, Cane looked like he wished Death would run a few red lights and get to him already. "Rosebud," he said. He was starting to cry a little bit. Rosebud looked like she was about to slap his skull across the room, when Ghost chimed in with a news flash. "Hullo," he said. "Could *this* be what the old boy is leaking about?"

We all turned and saw the Ghost of Christmas Yet to Come had pulled a sled from a nearby pile of toys. The rails were a shiny crimson and the board was a perfect plank of bleached maple. Across the middle, the word *Rosebud* was painted in red and gold. Cane lit up. He reached for the sleigh with weak, trembling hands when Ghost brought it over. He was happy, but I never felt worse in my life.

"Rosebud," I said. "I'm sorry. I'm sorry for doubting you, accusing you of all that rhubarb before. This whole thing has got me crazy. I don't deserve it, but I hope you can forgive me."

She didn't seem to hear me, but whirled back on

Cane. "A sled!" she screamed. "Are you kidding me? All that stupid 'Ode to a Lovely Rosebud' poetry you made me sit through night after night was really for a stinkin' sled? You better be lying, Cane, or I'm gonna get a doctor to revive you so I can kill you myself!"

"Um, Rosebud," I said and reached for her arm. She slapped me away and lit into Cane again.

"Your dying words better be that I was the best thing that ever happened to you and that you were stuck on me like spit to a stamp. I looked good for you, Cane. I wore hose! I made the effort to make you feel like the big, big elf! A girl doesn't slap on the war paint to be second best to something pulled by *dogs*, so you better change your tune before I make it so you whistle it out of your—"

"Rosebud!" I shouted. "The man's dying and we still don't know what's going on!"

"You're skating on thin ice at the equator, Gumdrop Coal, so shut your pudding hole if you know what's good for you!" she said and then whirled back on Cane. "Now, Charles 'Candy' Cane, spill every bean you got before Death's Kelly Girl here sings your final lullaby. Tell us who else is in this crazy scheme with you? Who set Gumdrop up? What are they planning to do to Santa next? What were you going to do with all these toys? And finally, tell of your great love for a cracker-jack reporter with a great brain, bedroom eyes and the gams of a Rockette. You'll start with the last first, if you have any sense."

Cane looked scared stiff because he was a stiff. Even in his weakest moment, the elf would have answered Rosebud's questions, or at least blinked, but Cane was as still as a church.

"He went early," Ghost said. "That's strange, but perfectly agreeable. I wanted him to snap things up, but you never really expect them to go before their assigned time. Of course, I can't hardly blame the sot, what with Jezebel here making staying so utterly frightening."

"He's dead?" Rosebud said. She gave Cane a frantic poke that would have sent most into the fetal position.

"Rigor mortis has taken up residence early and has its feet in recline," Ghost said.

"You say it's unusual for most to check out before their time?" I asked. Something was squirrelly.

"Oh, quite," said Ghost. "Most all hang on to dear life for dear life like something primeval would cling to a shank of protein, but Mr. Cane released a full five minutes early. Five more minutes he could have spent with his beloved Rosebud." If Ghost had had a face, you would have seen him smirk at that.

The nonsled Rosebud wheeled around and gave the phantom the evil eye. "You're quite the chatterbox, bub," she said to him. "I don't remember Dickens letting you yap so much. Now I know why. You're nothing but a big blabbermouth!"

"Sticks and stones, my truffle," Ghost said. "If Chuck would have let me meet and converse frankly with Ebenezer in the beginning, his masterpiece could have gone on the back of a menu. I could have illuminated quite clearly what awaited in Scrooge's future and booked his epiphany on an earlier train, but Dickens was paid by the word and wouldn't hear of it. He convinced me my silent brooding in the final act would boost the dramatic tension and endear me to fans forever. I have, however, discovered the opposite is true. Through stage adaptations of the work, fans have experienced so much ham in Stave Four, they tend to doze or skip pages until the Cratchits get goosed. I could have waxed poetically about the wages of sin and added a dash of brimstone to make things sparkly, but no. Through my cursed silence, most associate the Ghost of Christmas Yet to Come as a moody druid with arthritis. I blame them not, but how I would have loved to be allowed to speak. Or sing."

"Singing is where I get off the bus," Rosebud said, leaving. "Gumdrop Coal, I do not want to speak to you for a few days. I'm mad, bad mad. The idea that you could think such things about me makes me sick. The girl wants to be alone for a spell and wonder if you're half the elf I thought you were. See you around. But if I say 'go,' I mean go. Momma doesn't chew cabbage twice."

Dingleberry watched all of this quietly. Steady, solid Dingleberry. I knew he wanted to dig a hole in the ground and hide from all of this bad business, but he would never leave me, his buddy, unless I told him to. I told him to. "It's all right," I said. "I need to take care of something." I saw Dingleberry to the door and watched him go.

When I turned back, Ghost was pulling the sheet over Cane. "Wait," I said. "I wonder if the reason you didn't expect Cane to die so early is because there was a change in the cause of death."

"Heart attack is listed," said Ghost, but something told me different. I gave Cane the once-over, looking for wounds, but came up empty. I was about to give up, but I looked inside Cane's mouth. That's when I saw it. It had been lodged in his throat, slowly choking him to death and stopping his ability to talk. It was probably poison too.

Zsu Zsu's petals.

As I pulled the leaves out of Cane's mouth, I could hear the surprise in Ghost's voice. "What does it mean?" he asked.

It meant I was one unlucky son of a blitzen. It meant that Cane was murdered and I knew where the killer was hiding.

"It means I have to go to Pottersville."

CHAPTER 18

Baby, It's Cold Outside

THE MARSHMALLOW WORLD GAZETTE

Charles Foster "Candy" Cane Dead!

Deathbed Scandal Uncovers a Life Not So Sweet

Rosebud Jubilee

Kringle Town's Kublai Khan is gone. Charles Cane, nicknamed "Candy" for his uncommon sweetness, died alone in his fairy-tale mansion, Xanadu, surrounded by secrets, scandal and shame. The elf tycoon was discovered to have a clandestine stash of millions of toys. Though the investigation is in its initial stages, sources believe Cane's ambition was to stage a coup d'état and force Santa Claus out of the toy business. Authorities believe Cane then planned to become the giver of toys, the beloved elf of children around the world once Santa was disposed. Sources also told me that Cane used his considerable influence with Santa to remove Gumdrop Coal from duty. Coal was fired as enforcer of naughty children. With Coal out, all children would receive toys so production would have to increase, causing the elves to be hurried and less organized, and Cane was allowed to steal undetected. "I am very sad at both Candy's death and what was apparently a very selfish plan," Santa Claus said. At this moment, Cane cannot be directly linked to the murder of Raymond Hall and the other assaults connected to Gumdrop Coal, so the search for the fugitive elf continues. Although why anyone would ever want to see the good-for-nothing rat loser ever again this reporter cannot understand.

If I were an honest elf, I would admit that, deep down, I was maybe made to live in Pottersville. Pottersville was cold and bleak, sucking all hope and happiness into its shadows. It was the complete opposite of Kringle Town, my elf world in reverse. Just across the tracks, Potter lorded over the town like a buzzard, circling and smiling at the suffering down below. The old man took everything good in Kringle Town and twisted it into despair in Pottersville, creating a world where getting through life was an empty, joyless chore. In Potter's world, they would not exchange presents in *The Gift of the Magi*. They would exchange lead. The moon was big and full when I arrived, but it didn't add any romance to the view. In any light, Pottersville was ugly, crooked and in bad need of a coat of paint. But pastels would have been wasted on the place. Pottersville was quicksand to anything light or bright or happy. Because of my dark mood, the truth was that I felt right at home when I stood in Potter's Field looking at the sorry excuse for a town across the river.

I should have seen Potter was behind this all along. The warped, frustrated old man always hated Santa and would do anything to tarnish what the Fat Man stood for. Potter recruited Cane and told him to get me out of the way and start stashing toys. Then Potter double-crossed Cane and slipped him a couple of Zsu Zsu's petals as a funeral wreath. Genius. The worst part was that I was afraid once I was around Potter's scum, the pool and hooch halls with their hard hearts, that I would like it and never come back. My wonderful life, so called, wasn't doing much except kicking me in the duff and I was tired, real tired. If the wonderful life was going to be this hard, why not live in a place where the music and a bottle numbed your guts until it didn't

matter? Why not fade away where you could slap anyone who looked at you cross-eyed? I knew it would
break Santa's heart to hear me say those kinds of things,
but I was starting to feel like St. Nick was slipping. Before, in Cane's mansion, when I thought Santa was dying, I was scared, but a little part of me was glad that
all the trouble that came with doing good would be
over. And I felt a little something like relief.

I hated myself for thinking like that, but the cold
wind that blows through Pottersville cuts pretty deep.
It carries little voices that carve up your brain. "Rosebud doesn't love you," one said. "Dingleberry's a fool," said
another. "Santa's a bigger one." "The kids aren't worth
it," the breeze whispered. "You've always known it."
You stand in the wind long enough in Pottersville and
you start to believe those things. It was all I could do to
ignore it. I knew there would be no Angel Clarence, no
bells ringing and no toast to the richest man in town. I
was alone. Poor.

I was cold, so I thought maybe slapping the old man
around would warm me up. I couldn't find a path, so I
took off through the cemetery toward town, zigzagging
in the dark around tombstones and marble archangels,
trying to get to the road. It was a pretty bleak place,
gray markers, gray snow, so when I spotted some blue,
red and yellow on one grave, I got curious.

When would I ever learn?

The tombstone belonged to a guy named Van Doren Stern, but now he had company. It was Sherlock Stetson and someone had kicked the stuffing out of him. The old Misfit sleuth had a few pieces missing and his pull-string was wrapped around his throat. I wondered if this was the cowpoke the Ghost of Christmas Yet to Come was talking about? I wondered if Sherlock was really on to something with that Misfit Mafia talk. I wondered if Zsa Zsa knew her ever lovin' was dead and if she would finally appreciate his fine, sweet soul. I also wondered if I was imagining things or if whoever did this to Sherlock was watching me.

My gut told me to skedaddle.

Between the wind and the crunch of the frozen ground, it was hard to hear, but I was pretty sure someone or something was following me, so I walked faster. Whatever it was kept right up with me, darting to my left one minute, and then I'd hear it on my right the next. Because I was turning my head back and forth like someone trying to cross a busy highway, I never saw a thing until it was too late.

The next thing I knew, I bumped right into Uncle Billy.

This was not the "old Building and Loan pal" Uncle Billy. This was the Uncle Billy of Pottersville, the coot who'd been locked up in the booby hatch until the old man made him the town's watchdog. Uncle Billy even foamed at the mouth. He towered over me by a good three feet and he was dressed in rags. Colored, frayed strings were tied around each finger and thumb, causing Billy's appendages to turn blue from lack of proper circulation. I wondered if one of those strings was there to remind Billy to take Sherlock Stetson off the case. Uncle Billy's right eye gave me a wild stare while his left did a little jig in his noggin. "Boy oh boy oh boy! Where do you think you're marching to in a fine hurry on such a wicked frigid night, my little man, eh?" he asked.

"Hi, Billy," I said. "My name's Gumdrop Coal. I came from Kringle Town."

"Is that a fact, Mr. Gumdrop Coal of Kringle Town?" Uncle Billy asked. "Have you lost your way or do you have some denizen business within our tawdry streets?"

"I came to see Potter," I said. "Any idea where I can find him?"

"You came to see Potter, but Mr. Gumdrop Coal, Potter can't see you!" A switch had flipped and now Uncle Billy's face was red with temper. "Came to see Potter my aunt Fanny!" Uncle Billy stomped around in the snow and puffed a little bit.

"Listen, Uncle Billy," I said. "I didn't mean to rile you. Did Potter tell you he didn't want to see me?"

Uncle Billy discovered me all over again. "Who are you?"

"Gumdrop Coal. Kringle Town."

"Has the circus come to Kringle Town?" Uncle Billy asked. "Are you one of the magical midgets? Let's see a trick!"

"Not until I see Potter," I said.

"Ohhhhhh! You want to see Potter!" Uncle Billy said. "Of course you do, of course you do. Do you know where he is?"

Somewhere, deep inside of me, I heard a nerve say, *"I'm all you got left and the crazy man is on it!"* I took a breath and said, "No. Can you help me?"

Uncle Billy smiled like it was his birthday. "Oh boy, I might indeed, indeed I might. I know just the place to look!"

Uncle Billy may have been old and I would have hated to be hanging since the coot was sober, but he was as strong as an ox. He picked me up by the scruff of the neck and carried me down the hill to the road that led to the sad glow of Pottersville.

Uncle Billy's grip was pretty tight, so I didn't fight him. Being a passenger also gave me the chance to study the lay of the land in case I needed to plot an escape or hiding place. What I saw was a pretty sad sight. Most of the houses were dark shacks with broken windows and peeled paint. The yards were purgatories for junk and rotten trees.

As we tromped closer to town, I started hearing the

screams. That mean wind carried the sounds from every direction, roars of pain, sobs of regret and helpless shrieks. You could even hear the hushed weeping of despair and that was the worst of all. Kringle Town didn't have these sounds. When I delivered coal to the naughty, I admit part of me enjoyed the crying and the fits. But I really loved when those temper tantrums were later replaced by stiff upper lips and sturdy promises to do better. The joy of the season always overcame darkness; there was no stopping it. But for some reason, it was always midnight in Pottersville, an hour as lonesome and low as a lost dog.

As bad as the screams were, the racket of downtown Pottersville was worse. Uncle Billy turned a corner onto Potter Avenue to a jangle of loud music, yelling and car horns. Everywhere you looked, neon lights screamed empty promises of pleasure, like *Dance of the Sugarplum Starlets, Ice Cold Holiday Cheer and Beer, Mistletoe After Dark*. Pottersville citizenry rumbled through the streets looking for a fight or just coming from one. Your ears couldn't go a second without hearing a threat shouted across the sidewalk or the crack of fists and bones. The mob was a hurricane, tornado and flash fire all rolled up into one, spitting out little dark clouds of trouble to picnic on each other. I could feel the anger in my soul like a tribal drum. I could taste blood. If Santa died, I could survive here, I thought.

Then, I hated myself for thinking all over again.

As tough as the rabble on the street was, they made a path for Uncle Billy. Holding me like a football, Uncle Billy chugged through the crowd like the loco locomotive he was. The criminal class gave me the stink eye as we hustled by and, had I not been in the company of the town's nut uncle, I most certainly would have been fertilizing Potter's Field. But even the toughest hombres backed away from Uncle Billy. He was Potter's pet, dangerous as a rumba in a minefield. I was between a rock and a hard place, and it was about to get even less cozy. Uncle Billy pulled me close and opened the door to Potter's.

As soon as the door closed behind us, the ruckus of Pottersville switched off like a light. Potter's sanctuary had walls as thick as mountains, and the windows and doors must have been just as hardy because inside you couldn't hear a thing except the ticking of a slow clock somewhere. The floors were marble and walls paneled with huge slabs of dark, fancy woodwork. It reminded me of a coffin.

"What are you doing here?" Uncle Billy asked me. I touched one of the strings tied around his fingers and said, "You brought me to see Potter."

Uncle Billy smiled like an idiot. "So I did! So I did," he said and shuffled over to a set of doors just off the foyer. He turned back and grinned at me again and I felt my neck get clammy. Uncle Billy then pushed open the doors and there was Potter.

Dead.

Didn't see that coming. Where's Rudolph when you need him?

CHAPTER 19

A Warped, Frustrated Old Man

Potter's body was heaped on the floor like a pile of laundry. The wheelchair beside him was empty and eerie. The whole scene was about as charming as the mumps, but I didn't turn away until I heard the voice behind me.

"I see a vacant seat. A chair without an owner, carefully preserved."

I turned to see a sight that could only be seen in a place like Pottersville—Not So Tiny Tim.

The place across the bridge from Kringle Town warps everything and, in Pottersville, Tiny Tim was a hulking hunchback, a monster carrying a big stick. He limped toward me, dragging a bum leg and leaning on a crutch that looked like it could turn the Ten Commandments into gravel. He smiled like he had just burned down a church. "Gumdrop Coal," he said. "Welcome to the winter of our discontent."

"Tim, what are you doing?" I stammered. "What's going on?"

"Oh, I think you know, sir," Not So Tiny Tim said. "You said as much on the boat a few days ago. You just had no idea how far things had progressed."

The memory of the boat ride to Misfit Isle roared back into my brain. I remembered how I had teased Tim about being too nice for his own good, how he should use that crutch of his to clean a few clocks. I thought the little guy went quiet because of modesty. Now I knew that Tiny had crossed the bridge into Pottersville and turned into big trouble.

Not So Tiny Tim saw the light go on in my brain and decided it was time to get down to business. "Billy," he said, "Mr. Coal and I need to talk alone. I assume you were able to finish your assignment?"

A wide, sick grin burst out of Uncle Billy's face and he shook his head "yes" like it wasn't fully connected. "I did indeed," he said. "I did indeed. No worries there."

"Very well," Not So Tiny said. "Then you will find a bottle and a booth waiting for you at Nick's, Billy. With my compliments."

Uncle Billy was too excited to speak. He gave a quick little bow and hustled out the door without giving me another thought.

"I saw old Sherlock Stetson out there in the graveyard. Or what's left of him," I said. "Is that what earned Uncle Billy your compliments?"

"I'm afraid so," Not So Tiny Tim said. "The Misfit detective chose the wrong time to actually solve a mystery. I could not let him disrupt our plans."

"So am I next?"

"That, Gumdrop Coal, is entirely up to you," Not So Tiny Tim said. "However, based on the wisdom you shared with my good version back in Kringle Town, I hoped to compel you to follow your own advice and join us here in Pottersville."

"Why would I want to do that?" I asked, though I wasn't sure I wanted to know.

"To redefine the meaning of Christmas," Not So Tiny Tim hissed. "Gumdrop, you should be proud of the beating you gave Raymond Hall and that other rabble. You discovered the justice of practical thought and swift, appropriate action. My hope is that you have finally purged yourself of Kringle Town's diet of sentimental hogwash and will now savor a feast of power and influence that is served when you view the world as hopeless as it really is. Christmas should reflect that hopelessness and focus instead on getting what you deserve. And when the Fat Man is out of the way, we can do just that!"

Panic ripped through my gut like a bad burrito. "Tim, you don't mean that. Let's go back to Kringle Town, where you can get right again."

"Pish-posh, Gumdrop," Not So Tiny Tim said. "This is where I belong and so do you. In Kringle Town, Tiny Tim is a boring, pathetic Boy Scout who limps through the holiday pageant like vanilla eggnog. Potter gave me a talking-to a while back and pointed out that as a sinner, Uncle Scrooge was interesting, rich and respected. When he changes, the story is over. As Tiny Tim, I was tolerated, but only barely so. Following Potter, I crossed the bridge a few times to see if it was true. Every time I did, I grew up to the powerful man you see before you. Now, I command power. Furthermore, I believe you agree with our philosophy or you would have chosen to think that the goodness and kindness reflected by others would eventually influence and change the naughty. Instead, you chose—correctly, I might add—to beat them black-and-blue."

"I wasn't thinking," I said. "I made a mistake."

Not So Tiny Tim barked. "What you felt was instinct, natural. Those who can't behave must be punished. Those with the spleen and strength to punish earn the power to rule. You have that strength, Coal. The Coal Patrol is a perfect example. You just didn't carry it to its full course until you made an example of Raymond Hall."

"But I didn't kill Raymond," I said.

"So join us and learn how to finish the job," Not So Tiny Tim said. He shuffled over and opened the door to the ugly street. "This is your world, Gumdrop. These people would respect your ability. It's why you belong here."

Outside, the mob had formed a circle around two reindeer. The bucks were sharpening their antlers to deadly points, preparing for a bloody fight to the end. The crowd screamed bets to each other and waved wadded bills in the air. There was nothing like this in Kringle Town. I was taking it all in, when it hit me.

"*Us?*" I asked.

The hunchback turned and smiled. "Potter encouraged me to cross the bridge, promising me the attention and respect I deserved. But the old man did not thirst for power like I did. He did not know what it felt like to be a crippled child passed by Christmas's hustle and bustle. Limping and twisted, I could not hope to keep up while others pursued the perfect holiday, with Santa bestowing perfect gifts."

"So Potter was given the powder?"

"Precisely," Not So Tiny Tim said. "He did not have the proper motivation to crush Santa and the Christmas spirit completely. But someone else did. And I think you do, too. Your cravings for justice proved you would be a worthy partner. But when you did not kill Raymond, we needed a reason for you to seek asylum here. So naughty Raymond Hall got decked. A small sacrifice to call a lost sheep into the fold."

I felt like I was going to faint or be sick, or both. On one hand, I had been played like a toy piano. On the other, maybe the big hoss was right. If you can't beat 'em, join 'em. The world was going to heck in a hand-cart no matter what Santa did. I just didn't know if I wanted Not So Tiny Tim to be right. "Who's your part-ner?" I asked.

"Gumdrop, who else shares my affection for twisted ugliness?" Not So Tiny Tim asked with a big grin. "Who else believes the mean and the horrible should enjoy their rightful place in this world? Who has been cast aside? Forgotten? Looked on as useless trash?"

I knew. "The Misfits," I said. I felt like the saddest guy on earth. I didn't just need to sit down. I wanted to lie down in a hole and never get up again.

"I can't say that I blame them. Not after the way Santa treated them."

"So Sherlock Stetson was right," I said. "There really is a Misfit Mafia."

Not So Tiny Tim made a face that indicated that Sher-lock Stetson was spilt milk. "Sherlock Stetson couldn't find water if he fell out of a boat," he said. "There is no true Misfit Mafia. Just me and a few Misfits with a brilliant idea. Sherlock would have never had a clue of our enterprise had he not been married to the Misfit mastermind."

"Zsa Zsa's your partner?" I asked. I knew the answer, but I hoped I was wrong.

"A brilliant doll," Not So Tiny Tim said with true appreciation. "Santa underestimated her, which was his first mistake. Banishing her was his second. Once Potter brought us together, we became a force that cannot be stopped."

"So you're going to make the world even more miserable by dumping a bunch of Misfit Toys into it," I said. "Zsa Zsa and the Misfits get their revenge on Santa, and you are going to make the good kids feel forgotten because good as gold Tiny Tim was given the short end of the stick."

"See how easily that came to you?" Not So Tiny Tim said. "You are precisely right, Gumdrop."

"You'll excuse me if I look for the knife while you pat me on the back," I said. "I still don't know why I was dragged into all of this."

"Don't trouble yourself too much, Gumdrop," Not So Tiny Tim said. "It's a little more complicated. As long as the Coal Patrol was operating, there was always the chance that children would return to obedience and prolong the supposed need for being overly good. You should be commended for teaching children to show proper respect, but to try and motivate them to be good and nice continues to justify the need for a Santa Claus and foils our plans. The only one that could sell the idea of firing you was Candy Cane. For reasons that escape me, Santa was fond of that elf and could easily be influenced by him. So Zsa Zsa and I convinced Cane to have you fired, disband the Coal Patrol, and convince Santa to give toys to every child, naughty or nice. The increased production would weaken Santa's fortitude and compromise the quality of the toys."

"Creating more Misfits," I said.

Not So Tiny Tim smiled like he just heard a grandmother get hit by a bus. "Misfit Toys would be delivered to children all around the world, flooding Christmas morn with tears and anguish. And as time went on, people would start to take on the traits of their playthings and become twisted, angry and sick—just like that crowd outside! Beautiful, isn't it?"

"It's a peach," I said.

"The icing on a very sour cake," Tim said, turning to me, "was that one of Santa's own helpers started getting slaphappy with the believers, darkening everyone's view of Santa. However, since you seemed somewhat reluctant to carry through to the best conclusion—and since your guilt would leave Santa no choice but to forsake you—Zsa Zsa gave Raymond Hall the punishment you could not. Whether you ran to us for safety, or were caught by Santa, Gumdrop Coal, you have advanced our cause considerably."

Not So Tiny Tim was right. I could think the worst things possible and suddenly a beautiful, awful idea popped into my head. "The summit at Misfit Isle is a trap for Santa, isn't it?" I asked.

Not So Tiny Tim's laugh was hollow and dirty. "My dear Gumdrop. Pardon the pun, but that nagging conscience of yours is such a crutch."

CHAPTER 20

Haven't Earned My Wings

I guess the look on my face said it all: "I've got to get back to Kringle Town and save Santa!" and Not So Tiny Tim was having none of it. He gave a short whistle and the next thing I knew was that those two reindeer Tim showed me out in the street pointed their killer antlers in my direction and bounded toward me. I was about to be kebabbed by a caribou.

I like my guts to stay on the inside, thank you very much, and I wasn't going to give up so easy. So I ran. I turned into the dark maze of Potter's house and figured I'd find a way out, head to the bridge, cross back into Kringle Town and warn Santa. The reindeer had other ideas. I heard eight hoofs thunder into the house after me. I was in trouble and I didn't have much of a head start.

See, in Pottersville, there is no elf magic so I couldn't fly. Good intentions don't earn you any wings here.

Potter's place didn't give me many spots to hide, and the windows had bars over them. I managed to keep ahead of the reindeer ninjas because their hoofs slapped and skidded on the marble, but I knew I only had a few seconds before I was filleted. Getting back across the bridge was going to take a Miracle on 34th Street, as we elves like to say, and I needed a shortcut to that grand old avenue. So I took the stairs.

The route to the second story was a narrow staircase that twisted back on itself every few steps, chopping its way to the top. The staircase looked like it would slow the reindeer down a little bit, so I jumped up to the first landing in one leap and bounded up the rest of the flight as fast as an elf with eleven-inch legs can go.

When the reindeer took to the stairs, it sounded like the house was getting shelled. They crashed into each other pretty hard and got their legs and antlers tangled. As they scrambled to get loose of each other, I darted down the upstairs hallway and opened the first door I found. Big mistake, that.

The second I realized what I walked into, it was too late to turn back because a couple of sets of reindeer antlers pierced the door behind me like it was made of paper. The points coming out of the wood wiggled and bounced like they had a life of their own. Still, I think I would have preferred trying to outrun an antlerectomy instead of dealing with what stood staring at me. I had walked right in on the Pottersville version of Twelve Drummers Drumming. By the look in their eyes, I was in for a good beating.

The room was smoky and dark, but I could see that there were bongos and war drums. There were big bass drums, too, like you see in parades and drum sets reserved for rock stars. There were kettledrums and little toy drums no bigger than a cup. And there was one ragged old piece made from a hollow stump with a brown sheet of animal skin stretched across the top. It was strapped with a rope to a brown little man who pulled down his sunglasses to get a good look at me. "Say cats, dig what the dog drug in!"

"Our train done stopped at Square Town," said a drummer in the back.

"Wrong riff, short gator," said another.

"That ain't cool," said a third voice so deep it shook the room.

The brown little man held up his hand for silence. "Let's take five and catch his vibe," he said and walked over to me. "What's the jump, chump?"

I extended my hand and said, "My name's Gumdrop Coal. Is there any way out of this funhouse? As you can tell, I'm not very good at reindeer games. Just point me in the right direction and I'll get out of your hair."

"No can do, Scooby Doo," said the man. Then there was a rim-shot from somewhere in the back. "If the gimp with the stick is done with your shtick, you are out of bounds and the boss don't grease our mitts to let you give us the slip, dig?"

"That's a fact, jack," said the deep-voiced drummer.

"You're the Little Drummer Boy, aren't you?" I asked, trying to make friends in a hurry.

"Bur-rump-pah-bump-bahm!" he answered. "You got the name cool, but you're a fool, and that's the truth. You might as well turn around and face the music, amigo. Go back. March, that is." The Little Drummer Boy started to bang his drum to a marching beat and it only took a few seconds before the other drummers joined in. I could feel the noise all the way down to the bottom of my feet. The reindeer were slowly drilling their way through the door behind me and now the drummers were moving toward me. They all looked strong and they all had sticks. I noticed a door halfway in the middle wall to my left. Even if it was a closet, getting in it would buy me a couple more seconds, but I needed to distract the drummers. The only thing I could think of was to clap.

I went opposite the beat.

The drummers went BOOM.

I went *slap*.

BOOM.

Slap.

BOOM.

Slap. Slap.

It worked. The drummers were taken out of their rhythm, and they stopped advancing my way. Twelve hardheaded drummers started to bang away, each trying to establish a new beat, but what they got was noise. It sounded like someone had pushed a chest of drawers down the stairs.

"Bur-rump-pah-bump-BAHM!" shouted the Little Drummer Boy, banging his drum with extra emphasis. "Follow me, dig?!"

"No, I got the bass, baby," rumbled the deep-voiced drummer, pounding away. "Talk this way!"

The other ten drummers started blasting their own ideas. During the hubbub, I made a break for the door on the left-hand wall. If it was a closet, I was a goner. If it led back into the hall, I imagined I'd find Not So Tiny Tim and the killer caribou. As I jerked open the door, I tried to imagine which would be worse—and then I saw what would be worse.

It wasn't a closet or the hall. It was another room just like the first, only this time—wait for it—

Eleven Pipers Piping.

So this is what Potter had tucked away upstairs like some half-wit aunt—the mob from the Twelve Days of Christmas. Even in Kringle Town, this crowd was tiresome company, so I imagine Potter recruited them with the lie that on his side of the bridge, they'd be respected. The pipers didn't look any friendlier than the drummers, and some of them had dispensed with formality and exchanged flutes for lead pipes. They slapped the ends of their pipes into their palms with sick, hard thuds. Behind them was another door and I was pretty sure it would lead to the leaping lords and so on and so on, but the drummers were coming up fast and the killer reindeer behind them. I figured my best bet was to run as long as I could.

"Where do you think you're going, mac?" one of the pipers said.

"I got a hot date with the milkmaids," I said. "I'm in a hurry because I think a few of the lords have a jump on me."

"You think that's funny?" the piper snarled. "You one of those comedians that make fun of the Twelve Days, mister?"

"No, not at all," I said, stealing a couple more inches toward the door. "In fact, I've always dreamed of becoming a piper."

"Yeah?"

"Yeah. I mean, the drummers—that's not music. Any monkey can slap a stick on a table. And I can't be a leaping lord because I wasn't born to the purple, and the rest of the song is chicks and dames. No, if you want to be a part of the Dozen, a piper is the way to go." There wasn't this much tap dancing in vaudeville, but it seemed to be working. The piper handed me his pipe, "Give it a try, wise guy."

The flute was heavy and stout enough to bust a kneecap or ring somebody's noggin.

"You know how to work it?" the piper asked. Some of his buddies came up behind him and the others were heading toward the drummers' door to see what the commotion was about. The path to the next door was clear.

"Sure, I know how to work it," I said, lifting the flute. "You whistle into this little hole, right? You just put your lips together and *blow*."

With all my might, I swung the flute right into the kisser of the big piper and let the pipe do the rest of the work. And then I legged it out of there. As soon as he stopped seeing stars, I was going to have a passel of angry pipers and drummers on my tail and I needed to make some space.

Getting past the leaping lords was a cinch. The ten-spot of lords can't control their jumping. They are like a bunch of pogo sticks gone amok, and the only way they can really hurt you is if they just happen to land on you by blind luck. I used that to my advantage when I darted into the leaping lords' royal chamber.

"Someone has infiltrated the court, what!" said one

lord as he bounced by and into a wall. *Boing! Smack!* He had apparently kissed the wall many times. His face looked like a bad potato.

"Visitor ahoy!" cried another lord, who apparently fancied himself an admiral of the sea. He was dressed like he was going trick-or-treating on the poop deck. "Show your colors, man," he said to me as he flew by. *Boing.*

The other eight lords tried to steer themselves my way, but ended up ricocheting off each other. *Boing. Smack. Boing. Boing. Smack! Boing.* You could tell it hurt.

Suddenly, a piper burst into the room and was right beside me with a mean-looking flute aimed for my head. An instant later a lord fell from the sky and flattened him like a pancake. "Sorry, old boy," his lordship said to the piper. "Meant to get the other bloke." Drummers and pipers were now pouring into the room and leaping lords landing on them was my only chance of getting away. It ain't easy to run while looking up and behind you at the same time. The door to the next room couldn't have been more than ten paces away, but I had to dance ten miles to get there. The dance worked. The lords were out of control and the drummers and the pipers made for easy targets. I'd look up and see where I thought a lord would land and get someone to chase me to that spot.

SPLAT! THUMP! SQUISH! POW!

By George couldn't have planned it any better.

By the time I got to the other side, the floor was littered with wounded drummers and pipers and the oh-so-tough reindeer were too spooked to come any farther.

Not So Tiny Tim looked at the battlefield and smiled as he watched me go through the next door.

I guess he knew that, even in Pottersville, my luck with the ladies wasn't going to change.

But if I didn't try a little of the old Gumdrop charm with the dancing ladies next door, Santa was going to have a date with Zsa Zsa on Misfit Isle—and that was going to be a bad breakup.

CHAPTER 21

Dance of the Sugarplum Fairies

As I shut the door, the nine ladies stopped dancing. One of them glided over, locked the door and put the key in a place where only lucky keys go. She was beautiful, with skin soft and fine and white as the good dishes. Her hair was pulled straight back over her tiny, perfect head framing a face that belonged on top of a Christmas tree. She smiled and I felt my tinsel tingle.

Then she hoisted a leg as long as a country mile up in the air, and pointed her toe in a way that made you think of poetry. Eventually. As much as I hated tearing my peepers away from her face, studying that leg was nice work. And when she lifted herself across the air like a magic butterfly, the whole view got better, especially when she landed beside her eight other friends who were beautiful enough to raise the property values even in Pottersville.

Nine Ladies Dancing lined up in front of me like prize roses. Six inches behind me, on the other side of the wall, there was a mob of crazy trying to kick, scratch and bash their way through to tear me apart, but I didn't really hear them. All I heard was the soft *whoosh-whoosh* of the ladies' feet as they teased the ground with a kiss from their beautiful little toes. *Whoosh-whoosh. Whoosh-whoosh.* Like the ticking of a clock. *Whoosh-whoosh. Whoosh-whoosh.* The girls glided across the floor like a cloud, twirling and swirling in a song of arms and backs and toes and legs. Especially legs. They spun as quietly as a snowflake to the other side of the room and then stopped, and I thought my heart would break. Then they smiled at me, all of them. These girls were better fishermen than Saint Peter.

"I don't think I've ever seen something so beautiful," I said, trying not to gush. *Whoosh-whoosh. Whoosh-whoosh.*

I forgot what I was going to say next. It was just so nice there. Then, I remembered. "Excuse me, ladies. I don't want to seem rude, but is there a way to sneak out of this place?"

Whoosh-whoosh. Whoosh-whoosh.

"I don't want to leave. Really. But I have something I need to take care of."

Whoosh-whoosh. Whoosh-whoosh.

"I would come right back. Promise."

Whoosh-whoosh. Whoosh-whoosh.

I was getting a little sleepy. The past few days were becoming a blur and my eyes were getting heavier and heavier. Forty winks would do me. *Whoosh-whoosh. Whoosh-whoosh.* Santa would still be fine if I got there a couple of minutes late. He could take care of himself. *Whoosh-whoosh. Whoosh-whoosh.* Dingleberry and Rosebud could handle Zsa Zsa. They didn't need me. I'd just be in the way. *Whoosh-whoosh. Whoosh-whoosh.* Everything's OK. *Whoosh-whoosh. Whoosh-whoosh.* Santa. . . Sant . . .

Whoosh-whoosh. Whoosh-whoosh.

I don't know how I got to the street. My head felt like it was hatching an elephant and I could barely keep my eyes open. I reeled down the road like a kicked can. The street was empty, and as bleak as a spinster's Saturday night. Something wasn't right. The stores were boarded up, dark and ugly, selling midnight.

At the end of the block stood a little church. It was in worse shape than the stores. Someone was keeping sentry in a pool of dirty yellow light at the bottom of the church's stairs. It was a man, old and dirty. He was dressed in red rags and he hunched in the gloom by an old trash can. He was ringing a bell that sounded like it had the croup. It was Santa. A skinny, sickly, mangy Santa. There was no twinkle in his eye. His beard was clumped and gray. Santa didn't even have much of a lap to crawl into and whisper a wish. The Fat Man had disappeared.

I tried to call out to him, but I couldn't find my voice. He just stood there, ringing the bell, but the sound wasn't making a dent in the gloom. It just snuck down to the gutter to hide in the muck.

Then Santa noticed something. He lifted his eyes and stared hopefully down the street, like a sailor who's not sure if he's spotted land. Santa pumped the bell a little harder, trying to give the ring some joy, and stuck out his chest a little to show he was proud of his purpose on this sad little corner.

There was a family coming Santa's way, a mom, a pop, and a little boy and little girl who both looked to be around nine years old. The mom and pop had red eyes and tight jaws and each were yanking a kid down the sidewalk. The parents gave a sideways look at Santa like he was the last thing they needed.

The little girl pulled the pop up short. "Who's that, Daddy?" she asked, pointing at Santa.

"Shut up," the dad said and tried to yank the little girl along. "Move before I kick you down the street!" he yelled.

"But who *is* it?" the little boy insisted.

"Shhhhhh!" Mom said.

"I've seen him before," the little girl said.

"Me too!" the little boy said.

"Come *ON*!" the dad barked. Santa kept ringing the bell.

"Ow!" the little girl screamed. "You're hurting me!"

"Mommy!" the little boy said. "Who is that?"

"It's Santa!" the mom said in a huff. "Now let's go!"

"The junk man?" the little boy asked. Junk man?

"Yes," the mom said. "Now shut up and MOVE!"

Santa stopped ringing the bell and started to cry. "No," he said. "Not junk. Toys. I bring toys."

"It is junk!" the little girl screamed. She ripped away from her father's grip in a huff and marched toward Santa. "That doll you brought last year gave me bad dreams!"

Santa tried to comfort her, but she slapped his hand away. Then the father moved in and gave the old man a shove. "Back off, Nick," he said. "You touch my kid again, and you'll wish you had never been born."

"Please," Santa sobbed, "I only want to make the children happy!"

"By giving them guns?" the mother screeched. She had dragged the little boy into the fray. "Guns that shoot things and teach them how to be thugs and criminals?"

"No!" Santa said.

"Bang!" the little boy hollered, pointing a lethal finger at Santa. "Bang, bang, bang, bang, bang! You're dead, Santa! Dead! I wish everyone was dead." To prove it, the little boy gave his mom a fist to the stomach. Most moms would have wept if their kid had tried something like that, but not this mom. She kicked the little boy in the head until a goose egg got laid. Santa tried to stop her, but the dad and the little girl tackled Santa and started beating him right there in the gutter.

I was too late. Zsa Zsa and Not So Tiny Tim had pulled it off. I screamed for the family to stop, but they kept pounding away at Santa. I wobbled over, but knew I didn't have the strength to pull them away. The street was empty. I crawled up the stairs to the church door and pounded with all my might. "Help!" I cried. "We need help out here! Anybody in there? Where are you? Where are you? Do something!" But it was no dice. No one came out, no one heard. No one but me saw that family drag Santa's carcass down the street like a bunch of jackals. And there was nothing I could do about it.

I sat there on the cold steps of the church for an hour or more, hoping I would die. I was tallying up my mistakes against my good points and had a pretty good idea of what list I was going to land on. I thought I could make a difference with the Coal Patrol, but it seemed the kids grew up and were still rotten. I thought I could change the parents, but that bought me a stocking full of trouble. It just seemed that the whole Christmas cake was made with bad eggs from the start. It kept getting worse and now Santa was something to be hated because he brought them what they didn't want. The Misfits won.

I surrender. Better not pout about it, just try and forget it. Spilt milk.

Moo!

Now what?

CHAPTER 22

I Really Can't Stay

Moo!

Surely, I was confused.

Moo!

I was afraid to open my eyes.

Moo!

But something told me to be brave, so I finally took a peek. The dirty street and church steps were gone, which was good. But now I was face-to-face with a cow's nose.

Moo!

When I tried to jerk away, I realized I was flat on my back in a bed. The room looked like every room in Potter's mansion, except for the nosy cow.

Moo!

"What?!" I screamed at her. "Take a hike. What do you want?"

"You said something about spilt milk a second ago," said a voice from somewhere beyond the cow. "Ginger's just letting you know she didn't leak one drop. She's going for the record, you know."

"Moo!" Ginger said as a way of punctuation, and then slid away to reveal a woman on a three-legged stool. "You were talking in your sleep," the woman said, "and mentioned spilt milk. That kind of talk will get you stampeded around here, buster."

"I had a bad dream," I said, putting it mildly. "Let me guess. Milkmaid?"

The woman smiled. She had a sweet smile with a nice set of dimples. "Yep. And there are seven more just like me. My name's Butter, by the way."

"Butter? Butter Milkmaid?" I asked. "Does that mean you're sour already?"

"I still get my churn on, little buster, don't you worry about me one little bit," Butter said. The dimples were still there. Butter was a round mound of a real girl, all hills and curves, with hair as yellow as, well, butter, and eyes like the Fountain of Youth.

My whole body felt heavy. I tried to lift my head and look around, but I could have just as easily picked up a mountain. I couldn't see the other maids a-milking, just cows. Cows were everywhere, but it was quiet and peaceful. It was a nice change. "How come no one in here seems to want to kill me?" I asked.

Butter's dimples disappeared. "I hate to break it to you, pard," Butter said. "But you are indeedy going to get yourself kilt. They're just keeping you here while they can plan something extra mean."

"You want to fill me in?" I asked. "The last thing I remember was the Nine Ladies Dancing."

Butter picked up her stool and moved it closer, but before she sat down, she swept her foot across the floor in a graceful kind of way.

Whoosh-whoosh. Whoosh-whoosh. "Look familiar, baby?" she asked with a sad smile.

I certainly didn't need any more trouble than I already had, but I would hate to have been hanging since the time Butter had been at a dancing weight. She was in no danger of getting stalked by Ahab, but no one was going to mistake her for a sapling either. I decided to play dumb. "What gives?"

"That toe dancing in the next room," Butter said with a jerk of her head, "is how we hypnotize ya."

"We?" I asked. Butter didn't take offense.

"They," she said with a lonely smile. "I used to be one of them until I got too old and fat."

"You look swell to me, Butter," I said, lying in a nice kind of way. "If I didn't have a girl back home, I'd say it a lot sweeter than that, but you know how it goes."

"Don't I ever," she said. "Potter uses the Nine Ladies Dancing's charms to put a spell on folks, when he doesn't feel like having them beat by the drummers or the pipers. But when the girls get the least little bit long in the tooth for toe dancing and whatnot, she's made a milkmaid without so much as a how do you do."

I took a look around the room again. The other seven milkmaids were watching Butter and me. There were only seven there and Butter made eight. "Maybe I'm still soft in the head from the spell," I said, "but, after all these years, wouldn't there be more milkmaids than you eight?"

Butter's eyes went sad and she shook her head. "No honey, there's always eight and only eight."

"Then what happens to a milkmaid once a dancing lady moves in?"

"It's a daggum shame what happens, sugar, and that's the truth," Butter said. "We get turned into milk cows."

Moo!

Butter gave the cow beside her a kind pet on the top of its head. "It's OK, sweetie," she said to the beast. "You're still a beautiful girl, yes you are. As pretty as pie." Butter turned to me. "This is Ginger. Isn't she one of the most beautiful girls you've ever seen?"

"I believe she is," I said, knowing what was good for me.

Moo!

"Ginger says 'thank you.' See, that no-account Potter, in addition to running everything in this sorry town, has cornered the black market on white milk," Butter said. "Seems you elves just love your milk with your cookies and need plenty. Years back, Potter discovered that some elves were willing to pay through the nose for a little fresh cow juice, so Potter works us to the bone. There can only be Eight Maids a-Milking at any one time, but there's no limit on cows. When he turns a dancer into a maid, he turns a maid into a cow."

Moo!

"That's tough," I said.

"Tell me about it," Butter said. "I can't imagine it's going to get any better with Not So Tiny Tim in charge."

"Listen, Butter. That girl at home I was telling you about is a reporter. I'll tell her about the milk black market and she'll write a story that will blow the whole thing up. Rosebud's words are bombs and her powder is dry. She'll shame the elves who are buying black market milk. This whole thing will disappear like a desert mirage. I'll help her, I promise you. Just help me get back to Kringle Town. "

"It wouldn't matter," Butter said.

"Why not?"

"In case you haven't noticed, this town is full of car-
nivores and they like their meat rare and bloody. And
they're always hungry."

Moo!

"Besides," Butter continued. "You ain't gonna make
it back to Kringle Town, lamb. You ain't gonna see that
little girl and you ain't gonna tell that story. Not So
Tiny Tim's got other plans for you, and they're fowl."

"I didn't expect them to be pretty," I said.

"No, fowl, not foul," Butter said. "F-O-W-L. Potter's
gonna chain you up with the Five Golden Rings and let
the Seven Swans a-Swimming, Six Geese a-Laying,
Four Calling Birds, Three French Hens, Two Turtle
Doves and Partridge in a Pear Tree peck you to death
in front of the whole town. Kind of like gladiating with
birds. I ain't gonna sugarcoat it, sweetie, those birds
are plumb mean. The swans honk like a runaway bus,
the geese pelt you with eggs, the calling birds and the
French hens are pecking you all over, and the turtle
doves aren't doing any lovin', I can tell you that. And
the partridge is the meanest buzzard you'll ever hope
to meet. I've heard the last thing you'll smell is pears
and your guts."

"Maybe I could get my hands on some birdseed, an
anvil and a catapult," I said.

My joke managed to make Butter smile just a little
bit. "Sweetie, even Colonel Sanders couldn't save you."

"But you could," I said. Butter was listening. "You help me get back to Kringle Town and come with me. Ginger and the girls can supply milk for the elves directly and cut the bad guys out of the dairy business. And we won't work you too hard, either. You'll be loved, appreciated. I promise."

"What happens when a cow can't give milk anymore?" Butter asked. "We know what 'roast beast' really is."

"Nativity scenes," I said. "There are always churches and towns looking to borrow cows to act in live Nativity scenes, and Santa's always looking for extra livestock. Sure, Ginger and the girls may have to act for a few weeks with a bunch of hammy Methodists who don't know their myrrh from a hole in the ground, and some of the llamas can get an attitude because they are in such short supply, but it's an easy gig and no one gets put out to pasture."

Moo! Ginger liked the idea.

Moo! So did the other jersey girls.

Butter looked at Ginger and scratched the bovine's big ears. Then she turned to the other milkmaids and cows. No one said anything, but my plan had given them plenty of cud to chew on. "If you're lying to us just to help you escape, you'll be sorry," Butter said.

"Butter, I promise you will be happy in Kringle Town," I said. "No bull."

Moo!

She laughed. "What's your plan?" Butter asked.

"I need to ask you a few questions, first. And you've got to tell me the truth. My plan will take a little luck," I said. "And a whole lot of faith."

CHAPTER 23

I Can't Remember
a Worse December

If there was anything to make me feel chicken, it was the sight of swans, geese, calling birds, turtle doves and a partridge that looked like he could hunt crocodiles with a stick from his pear tree licking their beaks when I was led into the arena. We were outside in a stadium built just for bird bloodbaths. The crowd was roaring and their breath in the icy air made dark shadows across the big, bright, blue full moon high in the cold sky. The moon seemed close enough to touch, and you could see clearly it was not made of cheese. If it had been, it would not have been comfortable being close to so many rats.

The drummers and pipers were now sporting war

paint on their ugly mugs, waving their instruments in an unfriendly kind of way with one hand. Some were holding a leash on a Leaping Lord to keep the royal jumping beans from bouncing all over the stadium. Of course, Not So Tiny Tim was there. He was seated on a platform, high above the crowd, surrounded by torches and the Dancing Ladies. He didn't belong here. The sight of a ruined Tiny Tim would curdle mother's milk.

Just like Butter said, I was chained to Five Golden Rings. I had one on each ankle and each wrist and one around my neck. The rings were connected by a set of iron links Marley would have envied. I could only shuffle my feet, and I could barely move my arms and head. If my plan didn't work, I was going to be henpecked to death and Santa would walk into Zsa Zsa's trap. I hoped Butter didn't run into any problems. I hoped for a lot of things.

I made a wish on that big old moon. It blocked out half the sky so there were no stars available. The moon would have to do.

Uncle Billy led me out into the arena and the crowd got about as loud as a semi having twins. The swans started spitting and stretching their necks out, trying to appear taller and tougher. The geese circled above me like buzzards, honking and dropping big eggs from the sky, so everywhere I stepped there was a glob of yolk and shell. The calling birds worked the crowd, leading chants to increase the frenzy:

Short Time for the Elf!
Short Time for the Elf!
Heigh-Ho for the Dwarf!
Heigh-Ho for the Dwarf!

The Three French Hens were nothing like the birds I met headed into the Forest of Mistletoe. The three of them stood by a little guillotine and knitted, glaring at me like I had used the wrong spoon. Very French. I got a break with the Two Turtle Doves. They couldn't be bothered to get excited about killing me because they were having a little *Punch and Judy* show between themselves.

"I did not say you look fat!" said Turtle Dove Punch.

"No, you said I was fat!" said Turtle Dove Judy.

"If you would stop talking, you would be able to hear what I say!"

"I can't be talking too much because I'm too busy stuffing my face, birdbrain!"

"Just stop! Stop! You're not fat!" Turtle Dove Punch screamed. "Now, your mother, she's as big as a condor!"

"DO NOT TALK ABOUT MY MOTHER!" Turtle Dove Judy shouted back, and then she launched into

Punch like a blue jay with a toothache. The feathers were really flying, and beaks were getting bloody. The crowd loved it, but before they got too far, the partridge took his branch from the pear tree and whacked the turtle doves on the head.

"That's enough, you two!" Partridge growled in a voice that sounded like he was scratching something you didn't want to think about. "Break it up! We got a job to do." And then the partridge looked at me.

He was a tough little bird. The scars and torn feathers told me that he had been in plenty of fights, and the look in his eyes meant he won every one of them. He had this funny little waddle and skip move going; partridges don't really go high above the ground. The move made him look almost cute, like a kind of toy, but then he spoke in that voice. "I hear elves taste like chicken," he said.

"Not me," I said. "I'm past my expiration date."

The partridge didn't laugh. "A comedian, huh? You think you're funny?"

"Yeah, and I taste funny too." Might as well go out with a bang, I thought.

The partridge picked up his pear tree stick and waddled/skipped over my way. He fixed his eye on my kneecap and then *whack!* I won't lie; it hurt. Bad. I guess his boss wanted everyone to limp.

Not So Tiny Tim stood up and raised his hand to

silence the crowd. "That will be enough for now, Partridge," he said. Now the little forgotten boy from a ghost story was ready to make a speech. "Long ago, on a cold night not unlike this one, our world was deprived of its natural order by the birth of a child in a manger. This babe, friend of shepherds and the feeble, wrapped in dirty rags and surrounded by the stench of farm animals, treated the lowest like kings and replaced the impossible with miracles. By His touch, cripples walked again. Or *some* cripples. He left the rest of His work to a world that does not consistently, fairly reflect His philosophy. The result is that, in many instances, the weak, the ugly, the crippled are left behind without dignity or power. Until now."

The crowd gave Not So Tiny Tim a bloodthirsty roar, but the giant with a big stick wasn't done. "We, the ugly, the maligned, the Misfits are about to change things. The Child grew and taught that one should put others before oneself, to lose—on purpose. One such believer, Kris Kringle, was so hell-bent on reflecting the spirit of the Child's standard that he began making and giving toys to children all over the world. His only condition was that the children try and display the same commitment to the Golden Rule, so called, of being good, completely ignoring that they rarely appreciated the toys he gave. Santa also seemed oblivious that these children grew and filled the world with people who easily forgot the Misfits. And yet, Santa insisted that the toys he gave be perfect. It isn't fair, so tonight we are taking matters into our own hands. After tonight, Santa Claus will usher in the truth of the world at Christmas. The ugly truth."

Someone turned on a spotlight and pointed it in my direction. The light bounced off the golden rings like a sunrise and the only ones in the crowd that didn't cheer at the sight were too busy covering their eyes from the reflection. The feathers on all the birds raised up like hackles. The geese honked like tugboats and the swans hissed like cobras. The French hens knitted so furiously, you could see sparks fly off the needles.

"I want his head," said Turtle Dove Punch.

"No, *I* want his head," Turtle Dove Judy shouted back.

"We all get his head," growled the partridge, muscling the pear stick. "Because I'm gonna knock it into about fifty little pieces!"

I was scared right down to the ends of my curly elf shoes, but I wasn't going to give them the satisfaction. "Got any aspirin?" I asked with a smirk.

Not So Tiny Tim let the storm peak and then raised his hand. "What you see before you is Gumdrop Coal, a traitor to our way of thinking. He is loath to admit it, but deep down, Gumdrop agrees with us but will not embrace our mission. In his silly heart, he would still save Santa, save a Christmas that has 'perfect' gifts and 'perfect' memories."

More boos, but they were wrong. At the end of the day, Christmas was right. It was good. It was me that had the screw loose, but I didn't know how to fix it. I looked at the moon again, waiting for my wish to be granted. I was running out of time.

"Therefore, by the power vested in me," Not So Tiny Tim said, "I hereby sentence Gumdrop Coal to death, to be administered by the Twelve Days of Christmas Birds. Does the condemned have any final words?"

"Yeah. Shouldn't I get a blindfold and a peppermint stick in a situation like this?"

"You're stalling," Not So Tiny Tim said. "I have no doubt that you could nurse a peppermint stick for many Christmases yet to come. So no, face your death alone. Santa will not save you. Then maybe you'll believe the truth."

"Come off it, Tim," I said. "Come back across the bridge with me. Be that little boy that inspired good in everyone again. Tiny Tim has real power over there. Good power. What do you say?"

"You're a fool, Gumdrop Coal," Not So Tiny Tim said, but I could see I got to him. "What are you do-ing?"

"Hoping for a Miracle on 34th Street, I guess."

Not So Tiny Tim thought about it. I think he almost

believed that his former life had made a difference and
that he had taken a wrong turn. But the crowd started
to boo me and scream for my head. Not So Tiny Tim
gave me a sad smile.

"A Miracle on 34th Street, my dear little man?" Not
So Tiny Tim said. "Sorry, wrong number."

CHAPTER 24

Shakin' the Dust of This Crummy Little Town Off My Feet

It's true, right before you turn into a worm buffet, your whole life does flash in your mind like an old movie on the late show. I hope yours was better than mine. Prisoners would walk out of mine and gladly go back to their cell. Informants would rat out their mothers not to have to see it again. The big star was a miserable little elf, a real stinkeroo, and even I found myself hoping he'd get his. When Dingleberry and Santa showed up, the picture had some life to it, and you expected singing, but then the mopey star came back on the scene and it was time to go get some more popcorn. Rosebud only had a cameo appearance and I was sorry for that. I would have liked more scenes with her. Most of all, I wished the picture had a better ending. The fade-out was about to begin and then the credits would roll. I needed a twist ending.

Cut to a shot of the full moon.

Cut to a close-up of the star looking at the moon with a cocksure smirk on his face.

Now give the star a good speech.

I nodded at the partridge. "Have at it, birdbrain." That kind of language won't win any awards, but it kept the picture going.

The partridge didn't seem to like my attitude. With a flick of his head, he signaled the swans to attack and they glided over, hissing like vampires. "Well aren't y'all a bunch of ugly ducklings!" I said, but that only made them mad. The next second, a swan head butted me so hard, I saw little birds flying around my noggin. Before I could shake away the pain, one of the geese reached in and took a bite of my ear. *HONK!* The Five Golden Rings made it hard for me to move, so I tried to turn and dodge, knowing I had to stay on my feet. Once they got me on the ground, my goose was cooked.

The calling birds pecking my chest almost tickled, and for half a second I almost forgot about the lump growing on my head from another swan punch. But when the partridge slugged my other knee with that stick of his, I remembered to hurt. I felt like I had swallowed a running chainsaw and it was trying to get out.

There was a punch here, a stab there, plus a lot of scratching and biting for variety. Above the dull thud of punches and goose honks, I could hear the crowd cheer. I strained to hear the orchestra warming up for the final credits music.

HONK!

THUD!

"Don't look at me like I'm eating too much!"

"I wasn't looking at you!"

"Then quit looking at that swan! You think she's pretty?!"

WHACK!

HONK!

MOO!

Finally, a MOO. I might just make it out of Pottersville after all.

Ginger and the rest of the herd busted through the arena wall like it was milking time and the farmer had cold hands. Butter and the other magnificent seven milkmaids each rode on a big cow, whooping and hollering a stampede that ran over everything. Some of the drummers and pipers scrambled up walls to get out of the way. The lords' leashes were cut loose and they began to bounce willy-nilly into the stands.

At the first sign of trouble, the birds had stopped using me as a piñata, but one swan in particular was especially hungry and he wasn't going to let a little old stampede stop him. His neck coiled back like a rattlesnake and he aimed his beak at my head, but this time I was ready. As he struck, I put the chain between my hands in his way.

CLANK! The swan's beak snapped the iron like it was made of paper. My arms were free and one swan was nursing a bent beak.

Another swan cocked his head back to attack, so I grabbed a couple of calling birds off my chest and aimed them at the swan. When the swan struck, I squeezed the calling birds by the neck and they pecked the swan's eyes like they were on salary. The swan fell away and I tossed the two calling birds into the crowd. This was fun.

My feet were still shackled, so I hopped over to the French hens, tossing the other two calling birds at them like grenades. Being French, the hens skedaddled out of the way in a hot hurry and I slapped my foot chain under their guillotine and slammed the blade down.

CRACK!

I was free. Dingleberry would be proud. I looked like the hero in a *By George Adventure*.

"Hey, Gumdrop honey!" I heard Butter say above the din. I turned and there she was, riding Ginger. "Hop on. We're not out of the woods yet, sugar."

Butter pointed to the stands and I saw that Not So Tiny Tim was rounding up the drummers and pipers and pointing in my general direction. I took Butter's

hand and she pulled me up on Ginger and put me behind her. There was one bad-looking swan dead ahead,
its wings spread and its neck coiled like a cobra. Butter
looked over her shoulder at me and said, "Hold on tight,
darling. Momma's going through." Butter gave Ginger
a kick in the ribs and she charged. Cow 1, Swan 0.

Ginger headed to the nearest hole in the wall at a
full gallop with me and Butter hanging on for dear life.
The other cows and milkmaids pulled in right behind
us, blocking us from most of the mob, but the chase
had begun.

"We have to get to the bridge at the river before they
cut us off," I yelled to Butter.

"You are preaching to the choir, sugar," Butter said.
"Ginger here is running so fast we're going to be toast-
ing our escape in Kringle Town with milk shakes."

We galloped at full throttle, not stopping for any
lights. We had a pretty good lead ahead of the mob, but
there were side streets and alleys everywhere; it was
only a matter of time before something jumped out.

Drummers!

They skidded around a corner in front of us and
brought a few pipers with them to block the street.
They were a motley bunch, Yule Pirates, screaming and
waving flutes and drumsticks to beat the band. Getting
past them wasn't going to be as easy as mowing down a
swan.

"Any ideas?" Butter asked me, but my swash was un-buckled. If we charged them, there was a good chance that Butter and I would be yanked off and Ginger would be tenderized. The other milkmaids and cows might then make it through, and while it would be good for them, they wouldn't be much help when it came to going to Misfit Isle and saving Santa. As bright as the full moon was, it wasn't illuminating any escape paths on the dark street and my hope sank.

But then, the Lord works in mysterious ways.

The leaping lords do too.

They came bounding out into the street ahead of us like a house on fire, trying to help. But they were wild, launching off the sides of buildings like popcorn in a popper. Just like in the mansion, the lords rained down on the pipers and drummers like comets, crushing the menacing musicians like a jackhammer on an anthill. An instant later, the pipers and drummers were spread out across the intersection as flat as pancakes and the lords were arching back up into the sky.

"Go!" I yelled to Ginger. We had just a few seconds. If we could get the herd through fast enough, the only thing the lords would squash coming back down was the mob behind us. Ginger put her head down and ran, and the other cows were close at her hoofs.

The next thing I heard behind me was the wet, sticky *SPLAT* of a few swans and Pottersville citizens meeting the business end of a leaping lord's boot. It was a beautiful sound, giving us a little more distance. And we were going to need it too. I looked up the street and there were the Six Geese a-Laying waiting for us. By the stack of eggs behind them, it looked like they had plenty of ammunition.

The first egg caught me in the shoulder and lit a pain inferno! The eggs were hard-boiled, cooked to hurt. We were about to be stoned to death by a gaggle of geese.

But sometimes you just get lucky. You might remember in *A Christmas Carol* how the Cratchit kids loved chowing on goose, making a lot of happy noise when Momma Cratchit served up even the scrawniest bird. Years back, some of the Cratchit cousins had crossed the bridge to Pottersville, miffed that Dickens had not featured them in a sequel. The Cratchit cousins were the worst gang of hooligans you ever saw, closer to a pack of werewolves, but they loved a good goose too. The next thing I knew the Cratchit cousins—out for their nightly crime spree stroll—sprung out at the Six Geese a-Laying like an Apache war tribe. The geese never knew what hit them, their necks were wrung by cold, grimy, hungry hands. A second later, the Cratchits hauled off their kill to some dark cave, leaving nothing behind but some feathers and some geese grease.

Holding on to Butter, I tried to take inventory of who or what could still stop us as we rumbled to the bridge. I had taken care of the Three French Hens by hitting them with the Four Calling Birds, killing seven birds with one stone. I didn't know how many swans were out of commission and the Cratchit cousins had eighty-sixed the geese. I wasn't worried about the turtle doves because we could hear them three blocks over, lost and arguing.

"Turn left, turn LEFT!"

"I know where I'm going!"

"No you don't! Stop and get directions!"

"I don't need directions!"

That left the partridge and a handful of swans. If we got lucky, we might be able to outrun them and Not So Tiny Tim's mob.

We didn't get lucky.

Ginger skidded around a corner on two hoofs and then came to a quick stop in the middle of a junction where five streets spilled into a huge square. Coming out of the street straight ahead of us sat the partridge, feathers ruffled. The other three streets seemed empty, but the smirk on the partridge's beak made me hesitate. The little bird skipped forward a little and waved his pear tree branch at Ginger. "Try and run over me, you big dairy truck," he said, "and I'll grind your legs into chipped beef." Ginger took a step back and I can't say that I blame her.

I scanned the three streets for a trap. I couldn't see

anything, but I could hear the awful hissings of swans. But the sound was bouncing off the buildings and alley walls, so I couldn't tell from which street and how many swans there were.

The partridge gave a short little laugh. "I know what you're thinking. Did I kill four swans or five? Well, to tell you the truth, in all the excitement, I kind of lost track myself. But seeing as how if you choose wrong, there might be a hard-beaked swan ready to take your head clean off, you've got to ask yourself one question: Do I feel lucky? Well, do ya, punk?"

I was in a spot and the partridge knew it. I know I got a couple of swans when I busted out of the Five Golden Rings and the leaping lords mashed at least a couple more. Were there enough left to fill the three alleys? The Pottersville mob was closing in.

"What do you want to do, darling?" Butter asked.

"Any idea which street is a straight shot to the bridge?" I whispered.

"I think the one on the right," Butter said. "But wouldn't that be the one they block?"

"Or that is what they would want us to think," I said. "Go right."

"You got it, sweetie," Butter said. Then with her right hand, the milkmaid ripped off her bonnet and waved it in a big circle. "Forward, ho!"

Ginger blasted across the square, sparks kicking off

her hoofs. The rest of the cows rumbled right behind, pounding the earth so hard it almost shook your teeth out. By the way the partridge was swearing, I knew we picked the right street. I could see the bridge just up the hill. Once we crossed to the other side of the bridge, getting back to Kringle Town was a cinch.

But why make things easy? To this day, I don't know what made me look at the cemetery, but I did.

"Hold on a second, would you, Ginger?" I said. "Stop right here."

There just wasn't something right about leaving Sherlock Stetson to rot in Potter's Field. Even if the kids never cottoned to him, Sherlock Stetson was a good toy and a stand-up guy. I just couldn't leave him.

I zigzagged through the graveyard as fast as I could in the moonlight. Butter, the milkmaids and the cows were waiting for me by the road, and I could hear the mob roaring up the hill. I found Sherlock Stetson in a few pieces and scooped him up in a jiffy, careful not to leave any parts behind. I stuffed him in my vest pocket and hightailed it back.

"Heck of a time to pay your respects," Butter said. I had barely landed on Ginger's back before our cattle drive had kicked back into high gear with one goal in mind: get all the way across the bridge before getting caught.

But because I stopped for Sherlock, we weren't going to make it. I had worked enough Christmas Eves studying time, distance and speed to know that Not So Tiny Tim's mob was faster. We would get to the bridge, but they'd swallow us up halfway there and that would be the end of that. A few hours later, Santa would walk into the trap Zsa Zsa set for him on Misfit Isle and then the Christmas light would be snuffed out. There would be no more silent nights, or holy ones. Heaven and nature wouldn't sing; they'd gripe, cry and spit regret. In a few seconds, my world—the one I forgot to love enough, the one I thought wasn't fair enough—would be done. I missed it already.

But then I got a great reminder that Christmas was about hope and miracles.

The rope shot up into the sky. It was almost silver in the starlight, climbing higher and higher until the end of it spread across the heavens like a galaxy of good wishes. The rope unfolded into a beautiful ring and fell around the moon like a hug from an old friend. It was the kind of sight you wished for when you needed a friend. It was a whole hatful of wishes.

George Bailey lassoed the moon.

From his hiding spot in Pottersville, the real-life hero of *By George Adventures* gave the rope a yank and the moon drifted down as easy as if he were reeling in a kite. We ducked under the moon as we came onto the bridge and then George steered the moon between the mob and us.

"Thanks, George. I guess you are real after all," I said.

"Yep, yep, that's right, Gumdrop, I'm always around," By George said. "I'm kind of a top secret Santa's Helper. You know the old boy can't do it all, and he asked me to hang around and keep an eye on folks that need the most looking after. There are people everywhere, even in the darkest corners of our world, who need a second chance, and, you know, I believe everyone should get a second chance. They should get a third and fourth chance too. They should get as many chances as they want to live again."

I found myself grinning like Dingleberry Fizz. The best part was that we were safe. George hadn't disappeared. He hadn't built skyscrapers a hundred stories high, or bridges a mile long. He hadn't done anything for himself. The life he lived in *By George Adventures* was real. By saving the day, George inspired everyone to always be on the lookout for the other guy. It is a gift so simple, it's no wonder I didn't see it.

The worst part was that it might have been too late to share that gift. Right now, Zsa Zsa could be putting a stake of holly through the Fat Man's heart, ending the Ho ho ho in all of us.

Suddenly, there was a crack and I saw Not So Tiny Tim using all his strength to try and squeeze under the moon. Since he was still trying to stop me, I figured I still had a chance to save Santa.

"Take care of him for me, will ya, George?" I said, pointing to Not So Tiny Tim as I took off for Misfit Isle.

"Sure, sure, sure," I heard George say behind me. "You run along now, I'll tend to him. Oh golly, look! His mouth's bleeding!"

CHAPTER 25

But Santa, Dear, We're in a Hurry

SLAP!

Rosebud was still mad.

I met her racing down the bridge road on the Kringle Town side. When she saw me, my little tomato hauled off and rung my kisser like a heavyweight. "That's for going to Pottersville!" she said. Then she kicked me in the shin. "And that's for making me worry!"

There wasn't time to explain. I had to get to Santa.

Rosebud took off her boxing gloves and put on her reporter's hat. "What gives with the moon back there? Talk while you still have some teeth!"

There was no way I was telling Rosebud about George. He was Santa's top helper, a spy who went into the darkest places and gave folks a second chance. Sent by Santa, George is a friend to everybody, especially if you are at your lowest, and he had been helping the desperate across the bridge. When Dingleberry would go on and on about the comic book George in front of Santa, the twinkle in Santa's eye told me the wise old elf had something like George up his sleeve. When I asked Butter if George was the real McCoy, she trusted me and got a message to George. Together, they helped hatch the escape. But George was top secret. Ratting him out would put him in danger and his work was too important.

"A cow jumped over the moon," I lied to Rosebud. "Except she couldn't jump that high."

Rosebud was about to paste me again when Butter, Ginger and the rest of the milkmaids and heifers showed up. Rosebud arched an eyebrow at the cowgirl, but Butter ignored her and gave me a big old kiss on what I was sure was going to be my future fat lip.

"Thank you for everything, sugar," Butter said after giving me what I knew was the kiss of death. "I think our little adventure in the moonlight was plumb perfect!"

If Frosty would have been standing beside Rosebud right then, he wouldn't just be melted, you could use him to deliver a baby. "Butter here has got a good story for you, Rosebud," I said. "About milk."

"And honey?" Rosebud hissed.

By the time I got moving, I had a black eye.

I flew to Misfit Isle. It was the fastest form of giddy-up, and there was no more Tiny Tim to run the ferry. I didn't have time to worry about not having the Cratchit cherub around anymore because there was something fishy going on. The streets of Misfit Isle were deader than Marley's doornail. There were no Misfits milling about or even peeking from behind the shabby curtains in the windows. In fact, there weren't even any curtains in the windows. Windows and doors were boarded up and the streets were littered with Misfit junk that suggested that the whole place packed and left in a hurry. It was quiet. Too quiet. Of course, you have to say things like that in a yarn like this, but in this case, Misfit Isle really was too quiet. Fortunately, it didn't last too long.

"Hello, Gumdrop."

Santa! Beautiful Santa! Though he still looked tired and wasn't quite up to fighting weight, Santa was in front of me, dressed in red, with a white beard and a twinkle in his eye that was as warm and bright as Heaven's porch light. He was OK and I lost about a thousand pounds off my shoulders. "Looks like they canceled the party on us, my lad," Santa said. "I've wandered the whole island and there's not a soul to be found."

"You don't know how glad I am to see you, boss," I said. "There's a lot to tell you, but I think the smartest thing we can do is get you off this ice block as fast as we can." The place did look empty, but I had a feeling that all the Misfits were hiding somewhere. Waiting. It gave me the creeps.

"They're all gone, Gumdrop," Santa said. "Seems they had an idea that you were going to spoil their plans. I found this." Santa handed me a note.

Guten tag, my vittle Gumdrop,

I heard of your dashing escape. The news thrills me on one hand, and causes me much tears on zee other. To me, you have alvays been my pint-size helping of Manschnitzel, so learning of your bravery against zee birds makes my heart beat schnell. But I am also very sad because you did not choose to join me and zee big Tim kinder.

Vee could have been very happy, Gumdrop, a promise I vould have kept to you. But you have scorned me.

You hate Misfits just like everyone else. And before you come here to save Santa and foil my plans, vee are leaving, zee Misfits and I.

Vee vill find a place of our own, vhere vee don't have to depend upon zee mercy of Kringle Town. You do not have to hunt us, vee will cause no more trouble. But you von't have zee Misfits to blame for everyzing now. Vhen tings are wrong now, you vill only see yourselves—and vhat Misfits you are too.

P.S. I left another note for Santa and explained how I kaput Raymond Hall.

He now knows you did not do it. I only confess this because I have a heart full of love for my vittle Gumdrop.

Zsa Zsa

I had to read Zsa Zsa's note a couple of times to try and sort everything out. Her confession would end up in the paper and I would be in the clear, but somehow I didn't feel so free. Her words about hating the Misfits and being just like them gnawed at me and kept me from being happy because I wondered if she was right. It had always made sense to forget about the Misfits. The good girls and boys deserved the best toys. The bad kids got a lump of coal. That seemed like justice. But now I reckoned the Misfits were kind of in the same boat as naughty tykes. Maybe it wasn't their fault that they were messed up, but the bad kids could say the same thing about their parents. If my trying to teach Raymond Hall how to be a better parent was so swell, could I ignore how we failed the Misfits? Nothing seemed as simple as naughty and nice anymore.

"Gumdrop, I'm afraid I owe you an apology," Santa said. "I believe what Zsa Zsa said in her note to me is true and I am sorry that I ever allowed myself to think that you could have been capable of hurting a child, even a child that has grown up. Raymond Hall was, for the most part, a despicable boy and while it pained me to let you deliver coal to him, I only agreed because I believed it would help him learn. I think it did, in its way. Raymond grew up, became a father. He loved his children. That was his goodness."

"Santa, what would you say if I told you that when I delivered coal to the kids, and even when I started roughing up those bad parents, that I enjoyed it a little bit?"

The twinkle never left Santa's eye. "I would say you enjoyed it because you knew you were giving them a very special gift—the ability to learn and change. I believe that's why you enjoyed it, Gumdrop. It wasn't really the wielding of justice. That's just what you thought. Deep down, I don't think you enjoyed the violence; I think you took pleasure in sharing a lesson. Teaching someone how to learn from their mistakes—that's your gift, my boy."

I didn't think Santa was completely right. Part of me liked knowing the kids were disappointed Christmas morning, that I was able to get in their face with the lesson. When they sobbed and promised to do better next year, I scoffed. I thought telling Santa that might make me feel better, but I was sure it would make him feel worse and I just couldn't face letting anyone else down right then.

"Come along now, my boy," Santa said. "Let's give the Misfits' confession to that lady friend of yours to write in the paper and get ready. It's almost time for the Loading of the Sleigh Parade!"

CHAPTER 26

A-Wassailing

THE MARSHMALLOW WORLD GAZETTE

Do You Hear What I Hear?

Gossip with Butternut Snitch

Is it just me or when you were reading the Siren of Scoop's riveting article about how a certain outlaw elf was really a hero, you could almost feel the authoress blushing? I half expected to see "Mrs. G. C." written in the margins. I wonder if wedding bells will join the silver at the Loading of the Sleigh Parade and our hero will slip a cool breeze of ice on the reporter's nonwriting hand? I wonder if I'll cry! Stay tuned!

Dingleberry had read Butternut Snitch's gossip because he was staring at me like I had three heads. We were sitting in the Blue Christmas having a cup of cheer, trying to relax after all my adventures, but the notion that I might settle down with Rosebud baffled sweet, simple Dingleberry. Dingleberry was really the only other elf I had ever let get close to me, so I guess he couldn't figure me for getting hitched. I don't know where Butternut got her information, but I imagine Rosebud fed it to her to needle me. She had forgiven me for thinking she was in cahoots with Cane, but wasn't through making me pay for it. I figured getting my name in the gossip column was just another trick. Mind you, I wasn't opposed to the idea of Rosebud being my better half, but I hadn't really had time to think about it. I was thinking about it now and I suppose Dingleberry could tell. "Ding, you stare at me much longer, you're going to hurt your eyes," I told him. "The past few days roughed me up a bit, and I haven't gotten all my beauty sleep yet."

"I just can't believe it," Dingleberry said.

"Believe what?"

"That you would get married and not tell me. I'm your best friend, Gumdrop!"

Now I got it. Dingleberry's feelings were hurt.

"That's because there's nothing to tell, Ding," I said. "That story is all made up. Snitch is fishing or just putting things in her column to make people read it. Butternut Snitch lies like a rug."

"But you love Rosebud," Dingleberry said. "I can tell."

"Can you now?"

"Yep, you're different, Gumdrop," Dingleberry said. "Something is. I figured it was her."

Dingleberry was right about one thing—I was different, but I wasn't sure what it was. I was all mixed up inside. I used to think I knew what time it was. I checked the list, found the naughty kids and delivered coal. My life was that simple. But my world wasn't simple anymore. Coal wasn't the answer, neither was giving kids everything they wanted. Raymond Hall grew up and eventually got better. Tiny Tim grew up into a monster. It all depended on which direction they were shoved, when and who shoved them. I started out wanting to make a difference, but now I was all tied up in knots and I had nothing but thumbs. But there was no use dragging sweet, pure, wonderful Dingleberry into all of that, so I kept it light.

"I am kind of partial to Miss Jubilee," I told him. "And maybe someday there will be something to tell. And when there is, my friend, you'll be the first to know."

This seemed to cheer Dingleberry up a bit. "Good," he said. "It's not good for you to keep secrets and stuff inside of you. Even good ones."

"In that case, can you keep a secret, Dingleberry?" I

asked. "It's a big one, between you and me. You'll want to blabber about it, but you can't tell a soul."

Dingleberry's face got as solemn as a sermon and he nodded his head in the affirmative as seriously as he could. So I made his day.

"By George is real. He's alive," I said. "I've met him. He saved my life when I was on the other side of the bridge."

Tears welled up in Dingleberry's eyes and his mouth didn't know whether to gape or smile. "All that stuff you read in your comic books about Bailey being a hero is bona fide, and don't ever let anyone tell you different. He and his lasso are doing good things out there in the world. He's helping his neighbors and teaching the neighbors to do the same. Just like you do, Ding, just like you."

"Did you talk to him?" Dingleberry asked in a whisper, as if saying it any louder would shatter such a perfect notion.

"Just for a second," I said. "We didn't have much time in all the hubbub of the escape, but you know what he told me? He said, 'Gumdrop, please tell my old pal Dingleberry thank you. Thank you for making toys, for the *By George* fan club, everything.' That's what he said. You, Dingleberry Fizz, make Bailey proud, by George."

I've seen Dingleberry Fizz on a Christmas morning

when his toys get into the hands of a little kid. I've seen him when kids squeal and giggle and start making noises when they play with the thing that Dingleberry made with his hands and his heart. Ding's happy then, but at this moment, Ding was as happy as I'd ever seen him. But he was crying.

"I knew he was real," Dingleberry said. "I always believed. They weren't just made-up stories, parts of them were real. The good parts. I hope you'll read them now, Gumdrop, and see what I mean. I'll share them, I will. I've got fourteen boxes of books."

"I'd be honored, friend," I said. "Maybe that's how we'll celebrate the New Year." I raised my glass and Dingleberry clinked his. We were quiet for a few minutes, but Ding was restless. "Thank you for telling me, Gumdrop," he said. "But if you don't mind, I think I'd like to take a walk by myself before the Loading of the Sleigh Parade starts."

"I don't mind. I'll see you up there." I watched him go, bursting with goodness and happiness and hope, because believing in something had paid off for Dingleberry Fizz. Even though I saw George in the flesh and he saved my hide, doubt still gnawed at me. But Fizz was different. His faith was real. At that moment, I envied him more than any soul on earth.

I sat there for a while, stewing and chewing over everything. It wasn't long before Rosebud Jubilee couldn't stand being away from me. She climbed the stool beside me and pounded the bar. "Elvis, you old hound dog, you," she said. "My whistle is in need of a wetting. Oh bring me a Figgy-tini and shake it right here, if you please." The girl liked to make a production of ordering a drink, so I didn't interrupt the show. Rosebud also liked to make a lot of noise about pretending to ignore me. She slapped a copy of *The Marshmallow World Gazette* up on the bar so I would be sure to see the blaring headline.

Gumdrop Coal Innocent!
Plot to Frame Outlaw Elf Kaput!

Exclusive Scoop by
Senior Correspondent
Rosebud Jubilee

"Oh, did you want to see the paper, chum?" she asked me in a nonchalant sort of way. She was awfully cute when she was being annoying.

"I see the Nutcrackers are two games up," I said. "They're swinging the lumber pretty good right now, but their bullpen needs to be put out to pasture."

Rosebud took the jab and jabbed right back. "Well, then they won't be the only ones not getting to first base on a regular basis, I guess."

"Uncle," I said. "I can tell that you're too full of yourself today, so I wouldn't stand a chance. Elvis, put the lady's girly drink on my tab."

"Surrendering so soon, Coal?" Rosebud asked. "Not going soft on me, are you?"

"I was already soft," I said. "You're the one that made me such a hardened criminal in that little tale you wrote. I'll be the first to admit that I am prickly and persnickety, but you made me sound like Herod."

"But you come off a hero in the end," she said. "That's the stuff the readers want. So you *did* read the article!"

"Glanced at it."

"*Glanced?*"

"Skimmed it."

"Then you missed all the good parts," Rosebud said. "Looking back at the whole story, it had more red herrings than a Norwegian glutton. How did you figure it all out? Really?"

"Something tells me I haven't yet, and that's the truth." I turned to Rosebud to show her I wasn't kidding now. "I'm all mixed up inside, so maybe that's it, but something is bothering me that I can't shake."

"You take the cake, Coal," Rosebud said. "This caper is easier to wrap than a square box with good tape. Zsa Zsa and the Misfits are miffed at Santa and Kringle Town for giving them the stink eye. They find a sympathetic ear in Potter, he recruits gimpy Tim and they all plot to make it a Misfit world. But Potter is slow freight, so they push him off the choo-choo and chug along with their grand plan. They used you, Raymond Hall, Cane and a few others to try and rid the world of the Fat Man and Christmas spirit. They just didn't count on you having brains, brawn and—forgive me for sounding cornier than Kansas—a heart. That's it. Put a ribbon on it, it's done."

"Then why give up when they were so close?" I asked. "They could have nabbed Santa before I got there. Zsa Zsa had a pretty good head start. Why vamoose?"

"They're Misfits!" Rosebud said. "They can't think past Plan A. They ran and hid when they heard you got away. They went back across the bridge where they think everything and everyone looks good in the dark. Maybe it's where they belong. Let them picnic off each other, I say. We won't have to worry about them anymore."

"Maybe you're right," I said. "But I still don't get it. I want to know why all this happened. Why?"

"Forget it, Coal," Rosebud said. "It's Kringle Town. Understanding is overrated. Chew on something too long and it loses its flavor, like cheap gum, and then it's nothing but a sticky problem—and usually someone else's. Quit trying to know everything, sweetie. It will make you crazy."

"Er," I said and Rosebud gave me a look. "Craz*ier* is what you meant to say, but you were being nice."

Rosebud clinked her glass to mine. "Well, it is the holidays."

We sat there quiet for a while, watching the crowd at the Blue Christmas. Everyone was getting a little cheer before the Loading of the Sleigh Parade started and it was fun to watch the festive mood. Me and Rosebud would watch and then catch each other's eye and smile. Then we'd both look away quick, like a couple of kids. My head was empty, I couldn't think of a thing to say, so I made with the chitchat. "You going to the parade?"

Rosebud kept her eyes on the crowd, but her face turned the color of a Radio Flyer wagon. "I hear there's big doings going on up there tonight," she said.

Butternut Snitch. I just stepped in more quicksand. I don't know where the gossip girl got her story, but it wasn't from me. Was Rosebud playing me like I was the big fish at the end of her line? Deep down, I knew Rosebud was for me. I didn't need to shake the present anymore. I wasn't so sure I was ready just yet. I was thinking of all this and knew I had been quiet too long. I needed to say something. I could feel the heat on the back of my neck. "Oh, I'm sure something will happen," I said. "It always does."

No one can ever accuse me of being rude. I always invite trouble.

CHAPTER 27

Hang Your Stockings and Say Your Prayers

I've seen thousands of the Loading of the Sleigh Parades, but never get tired of them. Kringle Town puts on the dog and throws itself a big party. Everyone is there, happy that the hard work is done for a bit and that Christmas is finally here. There are bands on every corner, bells in every hand. Santa's sleigh sits in the town square, bright and shiny, and the reindeer look as smart as show horses. One after another, happy elves pile millions of presents into the sleigh. When you see the haul, you can't imagine how it all fits, but Santa's sleigh is a magical old rig; it never gets full. Even on a Christmas when naughty kids were getting gifts, Santa seemed to have plenty of room.

One of the big traditions of the Loading of the Sleigh Parade is the balloons. Elves make huge balloons of the season's most popular gifts and pull them along Saint Nick's Avenue with big ropes into the square. There are always giant teddy bears and baby dolls, so big that they seem to black out half the sky, but there are also new balloons each year, like race cars or spaceships or whatever the kids are asking Santa for that particular season. The little elves love to see the new balloons; their hands point up in pure excitement the whole parade long. Watch their faces a few minutes and you start to get excited yourself. Even a crusty, old, coal-delivering heart like mine softens watching a giant, bejeweled Princess Pony Cindy float across the clouds. Though I would hate to have to admit that.

Every balloon brings a new wave of cheers and music and squeals of happiness. Somehow they are able to time it so that the last balloon arrives just as the last package is loaded onto the sleigh. By then, it is dusk and the blaze of Christmas lights and candles under the purple North Pole twilight is one of the grandest sights in the world. You can get drunk just watching the stars rise and letting the happy sounds give your soul a good scrubbing. And just when you think it can't get any better, Santa steps out of the great hall.

As soon as you see the Fat Man, you don't know whether to laugh or cry. Most elves do a little of both, but this Christmas, the lump in my throat could have blocked a chimney. Santa almost didn't happen this year and some of that was my fault. Knowing how close we were to not seeing Santa step out in his red suit with that big smile on his mug made my eyes sting. Santa had been swell about the whole thing. "Don't worry about it, Gumdrop," he told me. "Everyone makes mistakes. You were doing the best you could. It turned out all right in the end. That's what counts! Here, have an orange." Something, though, still gnawed at me.

Despite all he'd been through, Santa skipped down the stairs like a kid on the last day of school, waving and Ho ho ho-ing like there was no tomorrow. The crowd was eating it up, cheering until the one and only Dingleberry Fizz started leading them into a roaring version of Gene Autry and Oakley Haldeman's rousing anthem, "Here Comes Santa Claus."

Rosebud Jubilee slipped her arm in mine and snuggled into my side like a missing rib. She looked up at me from underneath that darned hat of hers just as the words *All is merry and bright* danced over our heads. I took a deep breath and allowed myself to smile. Rosebud did more than smile back. She was a take-charge type of dame and wasn't going to let the moment pass without giving me a kiss so I would know what time it was.

Funny, during that kiss, time stopped. Happiness was a long stretch of road in the car with the radio on, the top down and plenty of sandwiches in the back. It was a perfect kiss on top of the world, full of the kind of mush that would make little boys squirm and old maids cry. It was good, better than I deserved, and I could almost let go. I vaguely heard, *"Hang your stockings and say your prayers,"* but I snapped to when I heard the screams.

There are a lot of ugly things in the world, but the balloon creeping over Kringle Town Square made you wonder if there was enough ugly left to go around. It was like a haunted blimp, cobbled and stitched together parts from parade balloons that had been discarded long ago. It had the tail from an old Hermy the Hedgehog balloon, a popular want from a couple of Christmases past. The body looked like it came mostly from the Polka-Dot Pig balloon, with a few patches of the Fur Troll Patrol balloon. Two legs were from some kind of cat balloon, another leg was from Ghost Duck. The final balloon leg was a long, tan, curvy gam that had been sawed off that Malibu doll. The head was the snarling, unfriendly puss of the long-forgotten action toy the Crocodile Cobra. The balloon that these parts formed was bad news and looked worse than any storm cloud. It was a Frankenstein dirigible. Even on fire, the *Hindenburg* looked better. But the worst part was what was in that wicked, hissing mouth of the Crocodile Cobra. It was full of Misfits.

The Misfits hadn't disappeared. They hadn't given up. They had tucked themselves in a balloon as ugly as they were, snuck right into Kringle Town and were now looming above Santa's sleigh like a nightmare. But it was worse. You can wake up from a nightmare. The Misfits were real and they were jumping up and down like banshees, ready for war.

Zsa Zsa stood at the tip of the Croc Cobra's lip, roaring like an earthquake. She had war paint on her face and was wearing a mean suit of battle armor with a sledgehammer in one hand and a rusty spear in the other. The Misfit army behind her was outfitted more or less the same way, all of them with wild eyes throbbing with hate.

Below, elves scattered like they were being thrown out of a bucket. The ones who could fly took off in a hurry, and the landlubbers darted through the square looking for cover. The ghastly sight had even spooked the hotshot reindeer and they just stood in their places with their mouths open, shaking their jingle bells in pure horror. And in the middle of the gloom stood Santa, helpless, doomed. He stared up at the Misfit warship as still as he could be. The only way you could tell he wasn't a statue was that statues don't have tears running down their faces.

"Are you waiting for an invitation?" Rosebud screamed. "Do something!"

I scanned the crowd for inspiration. There wasn't much. Halfway across the square I did spot little Ralphie. He had come to the Loading of the Sleigh Parade in his cowboy outfit, but now looked like he was wetting his chaps. But he was carrying his Official Red Ryder Carbine-Action Two-Hundred-Shot Range Model BB Gun with a compass in the stock. An elf's gotta do what an elf's gotta do.

"Is this thing loaded?" I asked Ralphie, jerking the Red Ryder from his hand.

"Y-y-yes," Ralphie stammered. "I'm not supposed to have it loaded, but sometimes I do."

"Good," I said, giving the lever a yank. "You might want to take cover, Ralphie. Go and get yourself a good hiding place."

"What are you going to do?"

"I'm going to blow that balloon out of the sky before it gets to Santa's sleigh, pilgrim," I said.

"You'll shoot your eye out!" Ralphie cried out of habit, but I didn't really hear him. I took aim at the balloon, but it was hard to keep the Red Ryder steady in the middle of the elf stampede. I needed a place to take careful aim, so I flew up to the rooftop of a nearby building.

Being closer, I could see the Misfit balloon was barely together, its seams were connected by a hodge-podge of string, ribbon, wrapping tape and Band-Aids.

All I had to do was find a weak spot and blast away. If I got it right, the Misfits would drop like a sack of hammers before getting to Santa's sleigh.

I didn't quite get it right.

I lined up the sight on the Red Ryder with an ugly seam on the front flank of the body and squeezed the trigger. The BB shot into the air and hit the seam, bull's-eye, and caused a hole to rip open, about the size of a bale of hay. But instead of a slow leak and sink, the balloon started zipping around the sky like a crazed comet, the hot air spewing out of the hole thundering like a rocket engine. The Misfit balloon was out of control: dipping, climbing, looping left and right, taking out Kringle Town roofs one second, big chunks of buildings the next. Elves were mowed down on the ground and in the air. In one whipping zigzag across the square, Dingleberry was scooped up right into the Crocodile Cobra's mouth and, a second later, was up to his innocent neck in demented Misfits. Santa, Rosebud and anybody who'd had the guts to look up before turned their heads to keep their eyes from being burned from the horrible sight. But anywhere you turned was ugly, heartbreaking lunacy and I had caused it. Somehow, I had managed to make things worse. Again.

I was mad and sunk. This had to be rock bottom. I ripped off my coat out of temper and to get ready for another fight. When I did, out came the parts of Sherlock Stetson I had picked up. The mangled little toy stared at me and seemed to be mocking. I ripped it to shreds and threw the pieces as hard as I could in every direction, but I was still mad. "Why does this keep happening to me?!?!" I screamed.

"Because you're doing it for all the wrong reasons," a little voice answered me. I turned, and sitting just as pretty as you please on the roof ledge was a little kid, about seven or eight, although he could have been younger because most kids that old were done with sucking their thumb and carrying a blanket. This kid did both, but his habits must have brought him a fair amount of peace because he didn't seem concerned at all about the pandemonium exploding all around us.

"What did you say, kid?"

"You keep messing up because you're doing things for the wrong reasons."

The Misfit balloon careened through the air and took out the Kringle Town clock tower, and bricks rained down on the elves that couldn't fly. I didn't have time for games. "Who are you?" I asked. "What are you talking about?"

"Why have you been doing all this?" the kid asked instead of answering. "Why do you do anything? For instance, why did you start the Coal Patrol?"

"To keep everything fair," I said. "The meaning of Santa wasn't getting through to the hardheaded bad kids. They needed a wake-up call, a kick in the rear. I thought there needed to be a little justice."

"How did it work out for you?" the kid asked.

"Don't be such a wise guy, kid," I said. "The Coal Patrol did a lot of good work. A lot of bad kids got the message and went straight. Justice served."

The kid worked his thumb for a moment and said, "True, some kids did learn the lesson, but the Naughty List kept growing, didn't it, Gumdrop? It wasn't as simple as delivering a rock anymore. Kids still needed something. So you decided to go after parents, didn't you?"

I didn't know who this kid was, but he was putting me on trial and I didn't much like it. "That's right," I snapped back. "When I got fired, I promised Santa that I would leave the kids alone, but I never said nothing about not cleaning the clock of a bad parent who didn't have the guts to jerk a knot in their own kids' heads. If the bad kid grew up to be a bad parent, they were fair game."

"And justice would be served," the kids said.

"That's right," I said.

"Sounds a lot like something you'd hear in Pottersville," the kid said. That stung. He looked below at the terrified elves and above at the out of control ship of Misfits ricocheting around, destroying everything in its path. "Kind of looks like Pottersville now too, doesn't it?"

From the mouth of babes. As much it hurt, the kid

was right. Looking at the square below, Kringle Town was as full of fear, confusion and anger as Pottersville ever hoped to be. The whole world was getting that way no matter how hard I wanted to push it back. I suddenly felt as empty as a forgotten cup in the desert. "Why?"

"Because you get more done with mercy," the kid said. "See, Gumdrop, when all you see is the bad, it is only natural to want to set things right, to make something just. But if you do that, what use then is the Child? We need the Child because none of us are worthy, none of us are really Nice, so there is His mercy. To need His mercy—and get it—is the greatest gift we've ever been given. His mercy, His love is what makes things right, not justice. Love. He came here on that starry night so long ago to give us the gift of mercy and love so that we could share it with each other, like so many Santa Clauses. Even though we should all be doomed to the Naughty List forever, His love erases our name from that list and there is no need for coal or justice. It's nothing we do. Pottersville is full of folks who have settled scores, but when you keep score, you never stay ahead for long. But if we really accept the Child's mercy, we truly change. The Child wants us to unwrap the gift of mercy every day and pass it on to others—especially to those who don't deserve it because that's all of us, Gumdrop. That's why the Child came. I said it before and I'll say it again, that's what Christmas is all about, Charlie Brown."

And that was all I needed to hear from the peanut gallery. There was something in my eye and it took me a minute to get rid of it, and when I did, the kid was gone, vanished into thin air. But that didn't matter.

It was time to do some good for goodness' sake.

CHAPTER 28

The New Old-Fashioned Way

Take it from me, brother, your guardian angel is
always just around the corner. Especially when
you're heeling the wrong side of the street.

—G. B., *By George Adventures*,
issue 359, *Lassoing Lava Lizards*

Back when I was a kid grunting through Black
Pete's elf boot camp, I would curse the little general because I couldn't figure we'd ever need all his
training. We were going to be toy makers, so why was
Black Pete constantly drilling us with flight training
and weights and leaving us out in the cold for nights on
end? As I soared toward the Misfit balloon, I knew why.
When I finally caught the towrope at the end of the balloon, I knew was going to need every muscle I had and
then some.

The hole in the side of the balloon was now bigger and causing the dirigible to whip and slash across the sky even faster. I could hear the Misfits screaming, trying to hold on, as their ship spun out of control. The rope I held was getting the worst end of the deal, whipping me back and forth across the sky, but I held on for dear life. Letting go meant an out-of-control flight into the wild blue yonder that no amount of elf flight school could help. In the back of my head, I could hear Black Pete screaming at me to hold on as I inched my way up to the lip of the Crocodile Cobra. When I got to the top, Zsa Zsa had other ideas.

Standing on the edge of the mouth and not one bit afraid of falling to her doom, Zsa Zsa put a boot on my fingers as I tried to hang on to the cobra's lip. "Vell, my vittle Gumdrop," she said with a sneer. "I alvays knew you'd come back to me."

"It's strictly a business call, Zsa Zsa dear," I said carefully. "Now, give me a hand and let's talk this thing out nice and easy."

"No, my vittle Gumdrop, I think I prefer that you die with all the zee rest of us Misfits," Zsa Zsa said. "I think that would be only fitting, ya? For even as an elf, you are a Misfit too. Vee should all go down together!"

A bunch of Misfits were holding Dingleberry prisoner, and he looked scared to death. The other Misfits looked spooked too, seeing the balloon was now cutting backflips. And not a one of them dared to try and cross Zsa Zsa to get out.

"It doesn't have to be this way, Zsa Zsa," I said. "I think I know how to get all of you Misfits into the hands of kids this Christmas. I think Santa will listen to what I have to say. I've had a big change of heart about bad kids and bad toys."

That got the attention of the Misfits in the balloon. They looked at each other with a mix of doubt, fear and hope. Zsa Zsa wasn't buying though. "It's a lie!" she screamed. "You vill only banish us to someplace else. You and Santa hate all that is not perfect, not nice."

"If I wanted to banish you, why am I holding on to this balloon?" I asked. "I'm trying to pull you back, but I need help. Dingleberry is a good flyer. Let him go, and together we'll help this crazy blimp land safely. Then, I promise, you Misfits will be on Santa's sleigh this Christmas Eve."

Zsa Zsa ground her boot down on my fingers until they were black. I could not hold on much longer. "Please. I've caused enough trouble. Let me fix things."

Behind Zsa Zsa, the Misfits were discussing my proposition and leaning toward believing me. But before a vote could come to the floor, Zsa Zsa lifted her foot off my fingers, kicked me in the face and sent me packing.

The kick stung, but what was worse was the helpless feeling when I blasted off into space, out of control. In that first instant, I went cold with fear and could see myself spinning and falling, not able to get right before it was too late. I wondered if I would pass out from flying aimlessly, or would it be more like turning out the lights when I blew into the side of a mountain or hit the ground? Nothing I imagined was appealing, but that's just how my luck was going. And then, in the very next instant, somehow, Dingleberry Fizz had me by the hand.

The Misfits had let Dingleberry go and, in a move pinched from *By George and the Skunk Pirates of the Gypsy Sea*, Dingleberry grabbed a Crocodile Cobra fang, looped around it a couple of times to build up speed and then launched himself over Zsa Zsa's head and out of the balloon's mouth. He beelined to me and snatched me from death's door before I had a chance to wipe my feet on the mat.

"I've got you, buddy," Dingleberry said. The next second, he handed me one of the towropes to the balloon and said, "Let's bring this balloon back to the parade."

Dingleberry double-checked that I had a good hold of the cord and then he leaped into the air and snagged another towrope. He wrapped the cord around his hand and gave me the high sign. "PULL!" he shouted over the rushing wind.

Like a couple of plow mules, Dingleberry and I bent into the air with the balloon ropes over our shoulders and flew straight down as hard as we could. If we could move the balloon closer to earth, the winds would be less, but it was tough sledding. The hole in the balloon was huge now, and the gas blowing still steered the blimp willy-nilly. But Dingleberry and I just kept at it. We'd gain a foot and then lose a yard, but inch by inch we were getting closer. When we came through a cloud, we could see an itty-bitty speck way down below: Kringle Town Square.

The sight gave me and Dingleberry a boost and we were able to tug at the balloon a little harder. Then we heard one last *pfffffffttttttttttt* raspberry behind us and realized that the Misfit balloon was out of gas and was just a big piece of rubber in the sky.

The Crocodile Cobra suddenly looked like it had swallowed a pit and shriveled up into a long, wrinkled raincoat. It started to drop fast and the Misfits inside screamed like there was no tomorrow. And if we didn't hurry, there wouldn't be.

"Grab the tail," I shouted to Dingleberry, "and I'll grab the head."

Dingleberry swooped through the sky and snagged the tail first, stopping the Crocodile Cobra's free fall. I swung over and grabbed a bump on the critter's nose and flew up until the balloon was straight and steady. Inside, the Misfits went from crying to shouting for joy. Even Zsa Zsa said, "Tank you, my vittle Gumdrop."

"Come on, Dingleberry," I said. "We've got some toys that need to be loaded onto Santa's sleigh."

As we cruised into Kringle Town Square, everyone from Santa and the elves to the reindeer and all the toys looked up, and no one seemed too thrilled to see us. Kringle Town was a mess with parts of buildings knocked to smithereens, and there were plenty of elves bruised and limping. Dingleberry and I brought the Misfit balloon to a soft landing beside Santa's sleigh. "Come out and stand behind me," I said to the ugly toys inside.

They did as they were told, pouring out of the mouth of the Crocodile Cobra like a bad meal. The Misfits were ugly and crooked. Some were missing eyes and some had mean-looking horns. But all of them, every single one, just needed a kid to play with them. To love them, and—like the kid with the blanket said—show them a little mercy.

"What's going on, Gumdrop?" Santa asked.

Here went nothing. "Santa, as much as I've been wrong about naughty kids, you've been wrong about the Misfits. We all have."

"What do you mean?" Santa asked.

"Santa, it would practically kill you when a kid went to the Naughty List," I said. "You knew there was some good in that kid somewhere, and good deserved a present. You were acting out of love, Santa, just like you should have been. I messed everything up with my idea of justice, of a kid having to earn your love by being good. We should love them anyway, no matter what."

"Yes, that's true, Gumdrop," Santa said. "And I think I can see where you are heading. That we owe the Misfit toys the same affection. But shouldn't good children get the most wonderful toys we can give them?"

"You're not giving a kid's goodness enough credit, boss," I said. "Kids, even the rotten ones, love toys. I mean, they are over the moon about them. Sure, the bratty tykes may rip the heads off dolls and turn even the simplest toy into a monster, but they *love* that monster. It's theirs. An ugly Misfit toy teaches a kid that being a friend takes a little more effort. You have to try harder to love it. Santa, you've always tried hard to find something to love in a child. Teaching kids to do the same with toys and each other is the best gift you can ever give."

The Fat Man blinked away a few tears. "That's quite a good gift, yes. In all my years, I've failed to look at it that way, Gumdrop. Thank you."

"Kids are wired to do good, think good, Nick," I said. "Or else there'd be no such thing as Santa Claus. Kids will play with anything, with anyone. It's the world that makes them stop playing. Maybe if we give them plenty to play with, they'll keep playing longer. I say, let's deliver all the toys to all the kids." When I said that, it seemed to change the meaning of "child's play" for me.

Santa was beaming. The Ho ho ho was ready to go. "And I am sure that if I ask the normal toys to play nice with the Misfits, everyone will have a truly wonderful Christmas!"

Right on cue, a Captain Chet Apollo action figure, bright and shiny, climbed out of the top of Santa's sack and slid down to the line of Misfits. The trooper put down his laser blaster and offered the hand with the orbit turbo ignition to a Misfit called Nutbreath the Flying Squirrel. "I'd like you to come with me, friend," he said to one of the stupidest toys ever made. "I'm going to a little boy that has an imagination so big, I'm sure we can have a lot of fun flying around the galaxy he creates. We'll do what we can to make sure you're not always the alien."

Underneath his gray fur, Nutty blushed and let out a hearty laugh. His breath could have knocked a buzzard off a gut wagon, but the trooper didn't flinch. "Yes!" Nutty said. "That sounds fun. Thank you! Thank you!"

"Ho ho ho!" Santa bellowed, and the whole square cheered. "Toys, find yourself a partner and let's finish loading the sleigh! We haven't got much time and I don't want to miss a child or a cookie!"

There was a mad scramble as toys found a Misfit to lead them to their place in Santa's sack. Everyone was smiling and cheering. The music started again.

Oh, you better not pout!
You better not cry!

Santa picked me up and carried me to a quiet place while the sleigh loading was finishing. He put me on his lap and gave me a pat on the back. "Thank you again for discovering this lesson, Gumdrop," Santa said. "But I'm interested in what brought about your change of heart."

I told him the story of the kid with the blanket up on the roof. About what the kid said about doing things out of love, instead of making sure everything was fair. How love, simple love, was what we should aim for and let everything else just fall away.

> He sees you when you're sleeping,
> He knows when you're awake!

"That's very wise advice from such a little boy," Santa said with a twinkle in his eye. "Tell me more about him."

"He was just a kid, Nick," I said. "Maybe seven or eight, nothing special, had a blanket with him."

"A blanket, huh," Santa said.

> He knows if you've been bad or good,
> So be good for goodness' sake!

"You know, Gumdrop," Santa said. "Sometimes blankets are called swaddling clothes. I'm just saying. You may have just had the best Christmas gift of all of us."

CHAPTER 29

Gather Near to Us Once More

All of that was a long, long time ago. I kept elfing for a couple hundred years more, and then decided to retire. It was time. I'd made a lot of toys, enjoyed many, many Christmases, and had been blessed more than I deserved. I decided to quit while I was ahead and let some younger elves know the joy I discovered. Santa said that I had earned the privilege of throwing another Yule log on the fire and to stay at home and do my best to drive Rosebud crazy.

Yeah, I surrendered. Rosebud and I got hitched pretty much after Misfits joined the regular toys in going to boys and girls all over the world. Santa officiated and Dingleberry Fizz was both best man and maid of honor. He cried like a baby, the little sap.

A lot of credit was heaped on me for the success of buddying Misfits and regular toys, but Dingleberry did all the heavy lifting. He worked up an entire formula for matching the right toys together and then putting those toy teams with the right kid so that now Kringle Town doesn't even see a toy as a regular or a Misfit. They're just a toy, a gift. They're something special. Only an elf with a heart as big as a house can do that, so when a kid squeals with glee at their present and learns to love it, flaws and all, thank Dingleberry Fizz.

Ding will never retire. He's busier than ever with the Toy Buddy Program and, of course, organizing the Kringle Town Comic Con and blogging about *By George Adventures* in his spare time. Rosebud and I don't see him as often as we like. Every once in a while, Rosebud will whip up some big feast (I insist on swan, naturally), and Ding will come over and we'll talk and laugh all night long. We're happy, but seeing Dingleberry Fizz raises our spirits even more.

Though times have changed and the toys are more complex than ever, Santa is still the same, jolly and bright. The Fat Man is back up to "shakes like a bowl full of jelly" and still gets a charge out of the kids' joy. The other thing I noticed is that, because Santa's gifts are made and given completely in love, the kids have changed a little too. Oh sure, there are still some little thugs out there who would gripe about anything, but in some magical way, the kids seem to really receive their gifts as something special, and that's not bad. Not bad at all.

My bride does a little bit of everything. She quit the paper after winning every piece of newspaper hardware she could get and turned to writing a series of mystery novels set in Kringle Town. The North Pole Noir series stars a tart-mouthed, peppermint-chewing investigative reporter named Lucy Lemonade. The dame is always stumbling onto trouble, but you can always count on Lemonade to solve the caper and lock up the bad guy by the last page. The books are as hot as sunburn, and Rosebud has been cranking out about a book a year with titles like *Rudolph and the Foggy Bog*, *The Mysterious Myrrh Maid* and *Love and Death—Who Capped Cupid?* Of course, when she is not beating a page of paper into pulp, Rosebud is full of secrets.

For my last birthday, she hatched a surprise party. Knowing I wouldn't go for such a thing, she kept it top secret, never even hinted that there were big doings going on. Turning older leaves me kind of grumpy because I tend to dwell on how many birthdays I wasted having that half-empty look on life. I was worse than half-empty because I was also sure that what liquid was in the glass was poison, so I kick myself for being stupid for so long. When I came home a few weeks ago for my birthday, I was happy to hear Rosebud upstairs pecking away at another mystery so I could sit down, relax and shake off my bad mood.

But before I could get good and settled, the front door opened and in walked Chauncey, the Farsighted Otter, a Misfit from the old days. I hadn't seen him in years, but there he was with a big bucktooth smile on his mug and his paws—all three of them—wide open. "Happy Birthday, Gumdrop!" he said and squeezed me like he was making Gumdrop juice. Before I could even ask him what was going on, a Chatterbox Wall Flower Doll came in and slapped me on the back. "Fifteen hundred years, huh?" she said. "You don't look a day over a thousand! Gosh, that's my little joke. You really don't! If I had to guess, I'd say you were about 700. Or 750. No more than 762 and three months, eight days. Do you like my hair? Maybe we can dance later? What do you think? Huh? Wanna dance later?"

Behind Chatterbox came another old Misfit, and then another. Pretty soon, the house was full of them, all laughing and talking, pumping my hand and giving me kisses. "I can never thank you enough for helping me find a kid that would play with me," they'd say. "Every day there's some new adventure!" "I've been passed down to three generations of youngsters," another would shout. "Once I was a Misfit, now I'm a family heirloom! Family! Can you believe it? Thanks for that, Gumdrop!"

I didn't think I deserved the goodwill surrounding me, but I actually caught myself smiling. That's when I saw Rosebud and Dingleberry up on the stairs looking down at the scene with big smug grins on their pusses. The big sneaks. Dingleberry pointed a finger at my bride and shouted, "Her idea, buddy! Don't look at me! Happy Birthday, friend!"

I blew Rosebud a kiss to let her know that it was safe to come over. When she got close, I could see she was trying not to cry, so I pulled her close and whispered in her ear, "I ought to wring your neck, doll face. But I think I'll kiss it instead." I did and the crowd cheered.

"I just thought you should be happy on your birthday for a change," Rosebud said. "You haven't wasted your time, Gumdrop Coal. You've made the most of it! Just look at these friends!"

I did and they were beautiful, but I just couldn't shake the feeling I could have done more if I had gotten smarter sooner. "Really?" I asked.

Before Rosebud could answer, all the Misfits started cheering again at whoever was coming through the door. The crowd parted and there stood none other than Sherlock Stetson.

The old cowpoke detective had been stitched back together. His stuffing was a little uneven and he was still as ugly as homemade sin, but that cockeyed grin of his beaming at me was almost more beautiful than I could stand. "Gumdrop, Gumdrop, Gumdrop, my good man!" he roared.

"Howdy, Sherlock," Rosebud said. "I'm glad you came, because I've got a bit of a mystery on my hands and I need your help." She jerked a thumb at me. "Hard head here wants to know why he deserves all this."

The clueless look on Sherlock Stetson's mug was the same, but since he had been the plaything of a very logical little girl, the little cowboy had picked up some elementary thinking. "Well, sir," he said. "Let me give you one clue."

Tiny Tim—who did not die—was standing in my door. He was a little boy again, with a shriveled leg and leaning on a crooked stick, but the light from his eyes made the stars jealous. Tiny Tim came back to us. The little boy in the big monster across the bridge realized what he had lost when he gave up on Kringle Town and Christmas. He didn't chase me in Pottersville to keep me there, he was escaping right along with me. Tim fought his way under Bailey's moon and, when George pulled him to the other side, Tiny Tim lived again.

"I'd like to solve the mystery, if you please, sir," Tiny Tim said.

"By all means, partner," Sherlock said with a bow.

"It seems quite simple to all of us, Gumdrop," Tiny Tim said. "You made us part of something. You made us something special. You helped teach friendship and love to a world of children, even the children who are damaged and twisted. They are, perhaps, the hardest to love, but you reminded us that they are who need love the most. Everyone will feel like a Misfit and be hard to love at some point in their lives. When one does, you don't want justice. You want a friend, someone who understands—a Misfit just like you. You helped children learn that friendship and mercy are stronger than laws and rules, that love, not power, is what lights the dark."

Rosebud sniffled a little and punched me in the arm. "Say something, you stupid galoot."

But I couldn't get my mouth to work. Finally, Sherlock Stetson came to my rescue. "Well, I reckon that solves the mystery."

I reckon it does.

Sherlock Stetson lifted his hat to me and bowed and the crowd yelled their heads off—a feat quite easy for some Misfits. It was a swell party and it went on until we were worn out from all the happiness. That night, I felt like I finally learned my lesson and could enjoy all my days, including the ones gone. I also knew this feeling was how old Scrooge was able to keep Christmas well and make every day that most happy day. You don't pout, you don't cry. Don't give up, give out until you're empty. That way, you can be filled up when something good as Santa Claus comes to town.

That's my story, and yes, Virginia, it's all true. I hope you liked it. I also hope that in your own way, you'll become a Santa Helper and spread the spirit of the season. You know what they say—inside everyone there's a Fat Man full of joy.

ACKNOWLEDGMENTS

This book would not have been possible without the support and good thoughts of many. I first want to thank Ben Sevier, Scott Miller and Melissa Miller not only for making *The Fat Man* possible, but for helping me make it better.

There have also been numerous friends who spared good wishes and encouragement for Gumdrop and the gang: Camille, Simon and Debbie, Nancy ("N.M."), Bob C., Brandy, Alexis, Tommy, Bob I., Trudi and every teacher I ever had. My sister, Karen, has cheered for me as long as I can remember, and I owe thanks to my parents, Bayne and Mary, for never, ever denying me books.

Finally, I am indebted to Kim and Luke who did not begrudge me the time I spent in Kringle Town—even when I was supposed to be doing something else. Thank you.

Ken Harmon, an award-winning advertising copywriter with a life-long affection for the noir novels of Dashiell Hammett and Raymond Chandler, is short and has a high-pitched, elfin voice. Combined, these attributes are the inspiration for his first novel. Harmon lives in North Carolina.